ALSO BY DONNA MINKOWITZ

*Ferocious Romance: What My Encounters with
the Right Taught Me about Sex, God, and Fury*

Growing Up Golem

DONNAVILLE

DONNA

VILLE

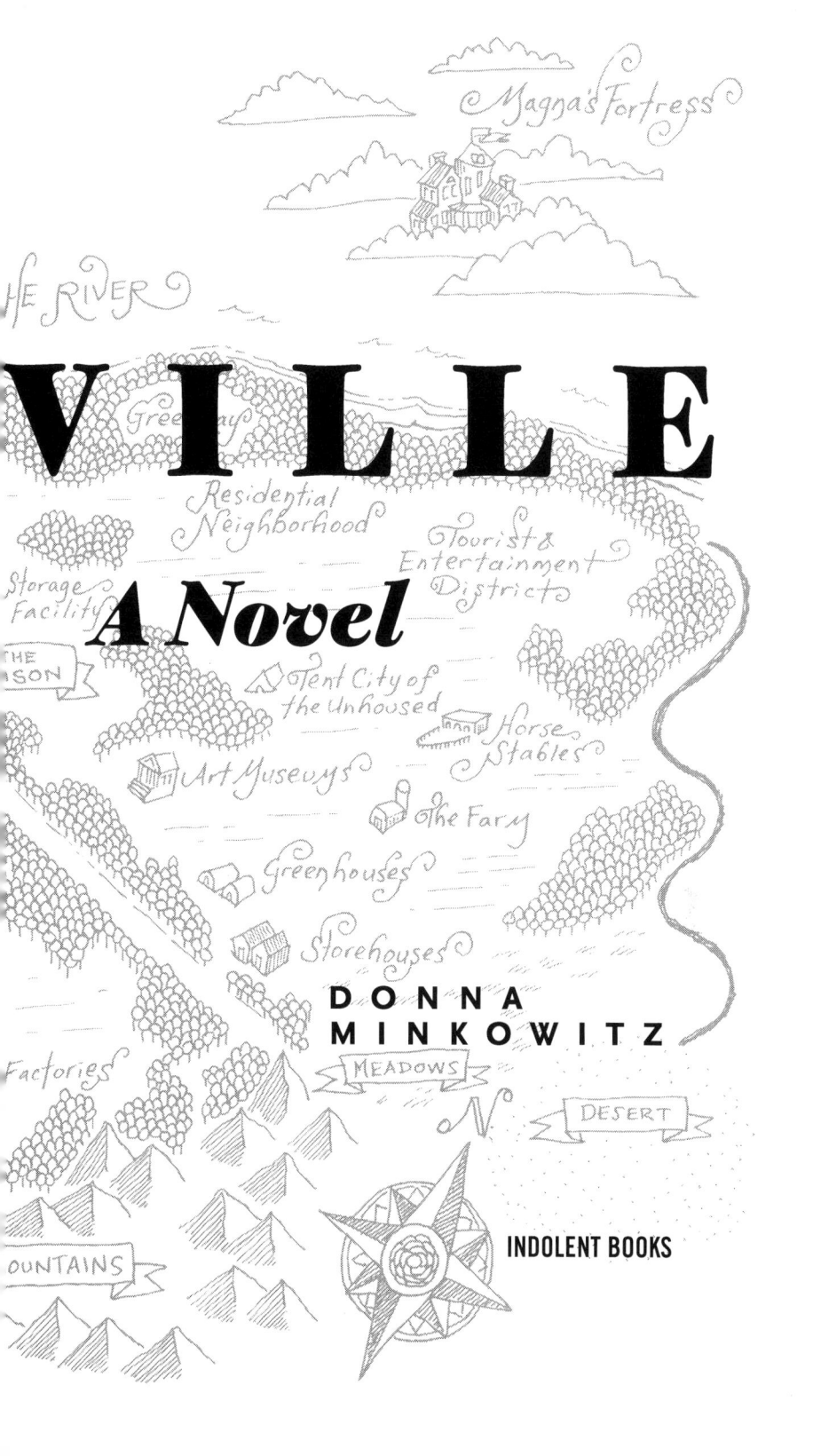

A Novel

DONNA MINKOWITZ

INDOLENT BOOKS

© 2024 Donna Minkowitz
All Rights Reserved
book design: adam b. bohannon
Book editor: Michael Broder
Cover art: Map of Donnaville by Brendan Lorber
www.indolentbooks.com
Indolent Books
209 Madison Street
Brooklyn, NY 11216
ISBN: 978-1-945023-35-4
Special thanks to Epic Sponsor Megan Chinburg
for helping to fund the production of this book.

DONNAVILLE

WELCOME TO DONNAVILLE

There's a room I've been coming to for 20 years. I hate this tiny, blandly-decorated room, yet I pay an enormous amount of money to enter it each week, like a professional dungeon. The room belongs to my therapist, Robin, a dry little woman with ditzy floral clothing and a cold sharp gaze. Her expression never warms to me, no matter how many years we look at each other, no matter how many intimate bits of myself I provide her to feed on. No matter how hard I try to make her like me.

She says she is not here to encourage me, or help me see my strengths. "That's not my role," she says, sounding like the voice of God.

Instead, she says, her job is to hold up a mirror to the places where I'm weak and wrong. "How long have you been coming to me, Donna?" she often asks, like an exacting schoolmaster.

Me (variously): Five years. Nine years. 11 years. 19 years.

"Then why are you still doing X bad thing?"

It's always the same bleak morning in the therapy room, and I have never learned what Robin is angrily, dourly trying to teach me: that the world is a hard place, that my optimism is misplaced, my confidence unwarranted.

Robin does not countenance tomfoolery. When I finally get up the nerve to tell her I wish our sessions were a little more playful, she frowns at me in distaste. "Therapy isn't play. It's hard work!"

She hates when I claim power, or act as though I can get anything—simply anything—without moving through a sea of pain. When I realize, for the first time in a lifetime, that I don't have to do anything I don't want to, and share this liberating insight with her, she just sneers, "Yes, you do!"

Beyond discipline, Robin wants me to learn normality. Not in my sexual preferences: she doesn't care about that. No, she wants me to be normal in my brain, in how I use language, the kind of things I say to her. She is distrustful of symbols, myth, metaphor, which are my mother tongue. My therapist always makes me translate myself into a bald, practical American idiom that admits of no nuance or double meanings. In the end, the only phrases I am allowed to share with her are stripped, flat, mechanical ones, the antithesis of the way I normally speak. Multiple-choice: "angry, afraid, sad, hurt, or happy," and I have to pick one. Only one. Robin doesn't like complications, or words that mean more than one thing. Nor will she tolerate my saying I'm afraid unless I can specify exactly what it is I am afraid OF. All subjects have predicates in Robin's therapy room. For her, psychotherapy has an iron grammar that must be respected. As a result, many times I am scared but unable to share it with her and be comforted. Not that Robin believes in comforting, anyhow ("That's not my role").

Finally, I have enough of giving up one whole day each week to commute into New York City so that Robin can erode my hopes and smother all my laughter. Something needs to change.

I can't believe I have given 20 years of my life, and thousands of dollars, to a woman who always makes me feel illogical, freaky, and wrong.

I begin exploring my internal landscape, which I have always guessed is wilder, more beautiful, and bigger than my therapist told me.

There must be a dank prison in there, true. But there is also a shimmery rose fluttering from within a cunningly elaborate bramble. There is a lush greenway along a river that produces toothsome oysters and succulent herring that may or may not be safe to eat. There are sprawling factories to the south that fire up metals at excitingly high temperatures, creating skyscrapers and staircases that go in all directions and strange, gigantic sculptures which some of Donnaville's armies of unhoused people have found can provide excellent, watertight shelter.

There are a fair number of blocks with blown-out windows, but the city is green and there are mountains you can see from almost every street.

The factories pollute the air, but Donnaville is situated in such rural environs that the air usually smells sweet. The wind from the mountains blows away the scent of butanoic acid, sulfur, and sodium bromide, except on a few days a year.

There is a lake.

There are sexy tourists who come to see the nature and buy toys from the boutiques in the glorious gentrified sections. (These also come from Donnaville's factories, some of the finest and most expensive children's toys in 500 miles.)

There are rich residents, and upper-middle-class residents, who try not to see what goes on with all the others.

There's not much I can say about the prison, except that you don't want to be there.

There is a jailer, a tense guy who I have a weird-ass soft spot for. He looks like he never sees the sun. There is a merrymaker called the harlequin, Donna's own master of beguilement and trance. The jailer cannot see the harlequin unless the harlequin wants to be seen. And so that scamp—an incredibly good-looking young man—moves through the city effortlessly, flirting, turning somersaults in the plaza, kissing dudes behind the factories, making fun of the cops, endlessly cool, and eternally in a state of enjoyment.

There is a goddess whose name is Magna, who is ridiculous. She is also so holy anyone would quake to touch her arm.

There is a child whose name no one knows. Donnaville's principalities and powers make it very hard to see the girl or touch her, but she lives in a precarious place in the city's dead center.

Welcome to Donnaville, where there has always also been a resistance. This is the story of what happened when that resistance took flight.

CAST OF CHARACTERS

This book is set almost entirely in my own mind, depicted as a city called Donnaville. All the characters are parts of me, except for the author's partner, E, and Hylas, a "tourist" character.

THE JAILER The jailer of Donnaville. The head torturer in the city's prison, as well as the prison's janitor. He can't remember his real name.

THE NARRATOR Donna. The author of this book.

E The author's partner.

THE HARLEQUIN Brother to the jailer. A trickster, liberator, and hedonist. He sometimes lies and tells people his name is "Bobby."

THE DIVINE MOTHER Part goddess, part memory of the differentiated good parts of Donna's actual mother. The creative and nurturing force in the world, she exists both within Donna and outside her. Her proper name is Magna, as in Magna Mater.

THE CHILD The city's most important prisoner. She is 8 years old and lives in the central, most hidden cell of Donna's prison. The description of the child in the prison owes a debt to a famous short story by Ursula K. Le Guin.

THE BROTHER AND SISTER WHO DWELL IN THE PUBLIC PLAZA Not biological siblings, but chosen family. Unhoused people who are anarchist resisters to the current regime.

V. MAEDDA A grocer who is part of the resistance.

HYLAS: A gay male tourist. He is visiting Donnaville on vacation. A genuinely different person from Donna, like E.

ANNA A lesbian baker of handheld apple pies. Skateboarding enthusiast. She emigrated to Donnaville in 1977.

CO GRAY The jailer's chief lieutenant. CO stands for Corrections Officer. Gray runs the prison.

COS SMITH, RATHBAUM, AUXILIARY PEPOWITZ, AND ANXIOUS Other prison guards.

RAYA, LESLIE, NEHEMIAH, SLOPPY, KHACHIYA Current inmates in the prison, along with Glenn (see below).

GLENN Former left-wing turned right-wing American political journalist who lives in Brazil with his young, adopted children and many rescue dogs. He used to write for *Salon*, *The Guardian*, and *The Intercept*. Glenn lives rent-free in Donna's brain, and within Donna's brain he is, naturally, incarcerated in Donna's prison.

SENSUALITY AND DELIGHT Two flying llamas who drive the divine mother's red wagon.

FALHÓFNIR A horse. A gelding with some unusual powers.

A YOUNG WOMAN, ALSO KNOWN AS KLEINE Donna in her 20s. Kleine evokes the German word for "small" as in "*Eine kleine Nachtmusik*" ("A Little Night Music"), but here it is pronounced "Klein."

MALA The mysterious keeper of a block of storage units. She rents them out to fellow unhoused people to sleep in.

VARIOUS VAMPIRES.

There must be a dank prison in there, true. But there is also a shimmery rose fluttering from within a cunningly elaborate bramble. There is a lush greenway along a river that produces toothsome oysters and succulent herring that may or may not be safe to eat. There are sprawling factories to the south that fire up metals at excitingly high temperatures, creating skyscrapers and staircases that go in all directions and strange, gigantic sculptures which some of Donnaville's armies of unhoused people have found can provide excellent, watertight shelter.

There are a fair number of blocks with blown-out windows, but the city is green and there are mountains you can see from almost every street.

The factories pollute the air, but Donnaville is situated in such rural environs that the air usually smells sweet. The wind from the mountains blows away the scent of butanoic acid, sulfur, and sodium bromide, except on a few days a year.

There is a lake.

There are sexy tourists who come to see the nature and buy toys from the boutiques in the glorious gentrified sections. (These also come from Donnaville's factories, some of the finest and most expensive children's toys in 500 miles.)

There are rich residents, and upper-middle-class residents, who try not to see what goes on with all the others.

There's not much I can say about the prison, except that you don't want to be there.

There is a jailer, a tense guy who I have a weird-ass soft spot for. He looks like he never sees the sun. There is a merrymaker called the harlequin, Donna's own master of beguilement and trance. The jailer cannot see the harlequin unless the harlequin wants to be seen. And so that scamp—an incredibly good-looking young man—moves through the city effortlessly, flirting, turning somersaults in the plaza, kissing dudes behind the factories, making fun of the cops, endlessly cool, and eternally in a state of enjoyment.

There is a goddess whose name is Magna, who is ridiculous. She is also so holy anyone would quake to touch her arm.

There is a child whose name no one knows. Donnaville's principalities and powers make it very hard to see the girl or touch her, but she lives in a precarious place in the city's dead center.

Welcome to Donnaville, where there has always also been a resistance. This is the story of what happened when that resistance took flight.

FRANK A gay man who is Anna's roommate and friend.

HANS AND SPLIFFY Refers to the unhoused brother-and-sister activists, above.

A RAT It lives in a Key Food in the west of Donnaville. Its name is Hornblower.

JASPER, CANTALOUPE, ESPARDENYA, MAGREET Four vigorous old people who live in the special neighborhood of Joe's Laundry in the west of Donnaville.

ALYIA Joe's niece, a powerful young woman who has just taken over running the actual laundry in that neighborhood after her uncle Joe retired.

THE BAD MOTHER Self-explanatory.

DAVID No information will be provided because this is a plot spoiler.

ZOSIMOS No information will be provided because this is a plot spoiler.

A geographical note: the city's topography is loosely modeled on that of Beacon, New York, the city in the Hudson Valley where the author lives. Donnaville's population is more than double that of Beacon, and its acreage is about 40% larger. The directions I call north and south in the book (toward the river and the mountains, respectively) are essentially west and east in Beacon (i.e., Beacon's map has been flipped 90 degrees).

CHAPTER 1

The harlequin enters the story singing: "*I am delicious! I am seditious! Super nutritious! Super pernicious!*" He chirrups in his candy-coated tenor, checking out all the men to the left and right of him. One has sweaty, tattooed Italian-American arms jutting from a tank top as he hoes a small bed of turnips, right where Donnaville's lone farm edges into its outbuildings. He imagines the man's pendulous dick curving inside his black jeans, maybe he should approach right now and.... Wait! Catty-corner to the turnips is a lanky brunette driving an ice cream truck, who looks like he might attend literary open mics when he's not out flogging strawberry shortcake bars. The harlequin likes his velvety eyes.

He's walking down the grassy road to the storehouses in the southeast of Donnaville, where the workers are hunky and the route beyond pleasant. Crocuses are coming up in orange, purple, blue all around the winding roads that begin at the farm. No one has ever yet refused the harlequin. They're all gazing back at him with interest, the turnip-farmer, the ice cream man, guys working a backhoe, when a strange thing happens. A thought slams into his consciousness: Raya, the prisoner that he tried to help last night. Raya looked unhinged when he found her chucked on the floor of her cell, scratching all over and crying.

The harlequin, lighter on his feet than anything else in Donnaville, has the power to zoom a mental sending of himself inside the prison and does so often to help those poor unfortunates in there and fuck with the powers that be.

So he did the wonderful thing he can do and shimmied Raya's mind right out of there, out of her fouled and bleeding body and the two of them played together among enormous starry fireworks of his own invention in a more beautiful sky than Donnaville's, and they smelled all the perfumes in the world together, finally choosing his favorite, vetiver, and hers, freesia, and smelling them alternately for a good 15 minutes, THEN, with a jolt, they were smacked back into the prison, where the guards immediately threw her body out on the trash heap. Her mind was no more.

He dashes the thought out of his consciousness. Rather like, although he's not supposed to think of it, the way the guards dashed Raya onto the garbage heap. That thought, the sad thought, is not supposed to be there. He is supposed to be ogling the fix-it men carrying their sacks of cement and farm-workers bringing melons and eggplants into the storehouse.

But why do things feel wrong? He is the most beautiful and the happiest person in Donnaville. No blemish will ever appear on his face, and his powers will never ever abate.

~

It hurts the jailer to walk, because it hurts him—daily, hourly, second by fucking second—to do almost anything. Lead is sewn into the bottom of his boots, ever-increasing weights of it at the toes and at the heel, so he will always both be slow and be in agony if he moves.

There are other little pains he has been provided with up and down his body, things that make it hurt to stretch his arms out, move his head very much, form his face into different expressions, jump or clap.

It doesn't matter. It will never matter, because he can take pain better than anyone else in this shit-stinking country. It is one of only two things the jailer has ever been good at.

Thank God, he can also *give* pain like nobody's business.

A rare smile crosses his lips as he drags himself across the threshold to the room where Khachiya is waiting, tied to a worktable. (She is a left-turned-right podcaster.) In the world outside the torture room, he himself always feels sour, acrid, twisted up somehow. In here and only in here, he can unwind. He always can relax in the room where his victim is waiting—especially such a deserving victim as this gloating, antifeminist little twerp.

In the middle of correcting her, a gap opens up in his mind. He is always alert, but for the first time ever he spaces out—ten seconds pass without his knowledge, after he's already begun hitting her. When he rouses, he looks down at the blackjack in his hand and can't for the life of him figure out why he's holding it.

The young woman in front of him is clutching her knees, so he comprehends what he's just done. But as he studies the mysterious object he is holding—long, made of hide, and absurdly weighted at one end—he can't imagine wanting to raise the thing. Can't imagine wanting to put it to somebody's flesh. Why would he want to hit someone with something so dangerous? Nervously touching the heavy end of the blackjack, eyeing the crying woman across from him, he just feels sad and a little empty. Odd. He is only used to feeling either sour, twisty, and nauseous, or else gleefully discharged.

∼

Magna is still in bed in the middle of the morning, looking down on Donnaville from the lovely fortress from which she flies down into Donna's city whenever she wishes.

She luxuriates with a cup of chocolate steamed in the Italian manner, laying her beautiful honey-colored curls back on the cushions. A coal-black sheep walking on its hind legs—one of the many animals that care for her—brings the goddess a sweet roll, butter, and honeycomb. No one has ever been able to make the divine mother feel ashamed about anything she takes into her body. She may have whatever she wants, whenever she wants it. She also can wake exactly when, or if, she feels like it. Or else delight in the wildest and most unabashed dreams the world has known. However, though she adores Indolence with a sweet, spicy, burning little passion, she also loves working. And strangely, Magna has just one thing in common with the jailer, her creation: She believes in duty.

Therefore, although she needn't do anything by a specific time, a small sigh escapes her lips finally as she gets to her feet, opens the huge arched window across from her bed, and, feeling a little foolish, gets into her special singing posture. She stands in a strong stance, her big feet planted, one slightly in front of the other, so her core muscles can support her lungs, her throat, her heart, and her voice when she begins crooning down into Donnaville.

But—most unlike her—she hasn't even begun her habitual chant when frustration overtakes her and—for a few seconds—she's so fucking grumpy she can't even open her mouth. Why is it always like this? She sings to Donna every single morning, and it never, ever works. Is she doing it wrong? Should she be singing something else? Should she be doing something else, not singing? She can normally do everything, so why can't she do this?

Frowning slightly, she steps up to the open window, still alive with the most luscious sunlight, and begins her song.

∼

Down in Donnaville, 100 miles down from the nurturing mother's fortress in the sky, I (Donna) sit outside at a birdshit-laden, plastic blue picnic table. I'm looking north toward the river, and savagely but halfheartedly ripping wax out of my ears. It goes like this: RIP! (Sigh and pause.) RIP! (Sigh and pause.)

Hey, I don't mean to gross you out: It isn't "earwax" (medical name cerumen) I'm prying out of my lugs, but high-end, delicate beeswax. More than 50 years ago I got hold of a large cake of the stuff, tore it into tiny bits, rolled them between my hands, heated and softened the bits before stuffing them in my very small, attached ears.

People are always surprised by how tiny my ears are, even as an adult. My body as a whole is very small, but my ears are ultra-petite. It's understandable I'm terrific at not hearing things that scare me.

Of course, I needed to put a thick coating of beeswax in there just to make sure.

Still—I'm ambivalent, but the time has come. I'm sick of this shit. I deserve something better. I want a parent inside me who is warmly loving. Whose greatest wish is to give me tender care. Not one who smacks me in the head and keeps smacking me. I want the nurturing mother to incarnate herself in me right now.

Oh come to me, goddess! I'm not exactly your type, I know, and Donnaville isn't exactly your temple, but please come here to me right now, underneath this apple tree in my yard. We can listen to the creek together glugging away in the background.

So, even though I'm not holding my breath for this to work, I sit at the table and scratch at the beeswax, layer by layer, bit by scented bit, and tear the stuff out of my ears that I wedged up in there years ago because it was so perilous to hear that molten gold voice.

~

The goddess sings:

Oh my Donna
my darling

I want to rub your shoulders
Oh lay down, lay your head down on my breast
I want to feed you
I have the food right here
a tuna fish sandwich
and a meatball one

and I have roses for you so you will always know
how wonderful you are

my delight, my little cookie
my bright animal

my brave girl
full of fire

and I will spread around you all that you might ever have needed
all you might ever love

baby

By this point, I can smell her perfume, and almost see the long silk scarf she wears, the color of saffron. She has almost incarnated here on the picnic table across from me, and as her form wavers in the noontime light I feel drunk and terrified at the same time. Her satiny dress underneath the table barely touches my leg.

"I will never leave you," she says loudly—warm hand heavy on my shoulder—and I turn away, squinching my eyes towards the neighbor's house, and whisper very low (inside my own head), "Please." Her nipple enters my mouth, bright red, it pops inside, I have never felt anything so heavenly, but what I mutter in the direction of the neighbor's house is "Please. I cannot bear your betrayal."

∽

Also down in Donnaville, in an iron room the divine mother can never enter, someone imagines someone saying a soft word to them. The person imagining is eight years old, and currently cringing in a pile of dirty straw in the most secure, the most hidden and best-defended place in Donnaville. This safe room, however, is not safe. Every couple of days the jailer comes in and beats the child around the head, kidneys, and knees and then feeds it. The food and the beating always goes together. Sometimes it is varied and he beats her around the shoulders, breastbone, and genitals. The jailer considers his work with the child his most profound responsibility, the corrective and protective foundation without which the entire edifice of Donnaville will fail.

The child's cell is sometimes very hot and sometimes very cold, and smells like a hamster cage. The divine mother has never been able to get inside the child's cell, for it is barred to her, but the child imagines (remembers?) someone, some lady, speaking to her, remembers a pleasant sound. The jailer has not been there in a few days, and the child is crazy hungry. Beyond that, she actually misses the man. She cares for the weird, terrifying, pinched-up jailer, who is the only person she usually sees.

Still, she is imagining right now that she hears something beautiful. So the little girl inclines her ears, stretching her hearing to all four iron walls, and beyond them, stretching them to find the sound.

∾

Of course, no one is exactly leaping forward to relieve the jailer of his responsibilities, just because he had a funny feeling in the torture room.

Soon, he's going to have to do the next prisoners on his roster.

But what if his problem happens again?

He's frightened what the punishment would be.

He ducks into his room (for he lives in the jail) and crashes onto his tiny iron cot. The floor is dusty, and there are fleas under the bed, in the floorboards. Not much else in the room. He dashes for an enormous two-handled jug on the floor (made of a lead-based pewter) and chugs it down. He drinks milk every day, because he is intolerant of it. He has to learn composure in the face of adversity, and this does the trick. It makes him break out in hives and have diarrhea.

∼

The greenhouses are prolific, because Donna feels compensated by having out-of-season fruits and vegetables available whenever possible. It's an impulse the harlequin heartily endorses. It is only his power that makes it happen, for he is something like a god. He brings his glamour to bear on the bulging of papayas and figs, the brooding ripeness of blackberries, the mysterious scent of citrus that wafts over the city even when it's shackled in winter, and the guards drag citizens over the ice and up the little stairs into the prison.

But even though today is a holy time, the eve of the spring equinox, the harlequin's cruising at the hothouses was weirdly unrewarding this morning. Despite the fact that the farm is staffed by some of the most electrifying bodies in the city.

The harlequin always makes out. But today, though he enjoyed looking at men as always, he connected with exactly none of them. It's not that he was rejected—as I say, this has never yet happened—but he simply had no urge to get with any of them. Even the beautiful willowy femme boy climbing up on a roof, displaying long, lithe, hairless legs, even the jacked shorty making a pile of bursting yellow peaches on a low table.

He feels hollow, spurious somehow, like there is a giant hole inside through which his affable, puckish personality has come pouring out on the ground like nothing. When he is used to feeling ever-expansive, indomitable, magical, suave, and oh yeah, hard.

∽

The harlequin returns to his digs in the very south of Donnaville, in the mountains where no one goes.

Let us spy on him at home, something no one else has managed to do to date.

His home is a tiny black thing, fitted like a ship. There are no windows. The ship is round, like a nut. It just might be that the harlequin, like one of Shakespeare's fairies, lives in a nut. That nut is also a Faraday cage.

A Faraday cage is an enclosure that prevents electromagnetic energy from getting in. It is not, properly speaking, a cage but a protected sphere. Nothing can harm him here.

The harlequin speaks: I'm in my nut. The walls are beautiful and black.

There is nothing here to bother me. The black walls shine. There are no doors. Where I live is like a jewel.

In his round home, the harlequin lies gloriously naked and spreadeagled. There is just enough room in his shining black jewel to stretch out his arms and legs in every direction. He believes he draws energy into him from the universe through his limbs, but in fact energy is precisely what cannot get inside these walls. There is also no food, no water, and not a soul to talk to. There is not even a bed. There is only a black shell.

∾

When I was in fifth grade, I had a recurring fantasy:

First my eyes pop off, then my nose. Then all my teeth pop out, softly and easily. There is no violence or sickness to any of this, only sweet relief.

Then my ears come off. It is so peaceful. Then I put my head under a hill, forever.

∾

After the milk, the jailer steels himself, then looks at his list again: HA! The next name on the list is Donna.

He doesn't know what's been happening to him this morning, but *that* bitch, *that* bitch has it coming. He's not going to have any problems.

He can't anticipate any trouble whatsoever. His arms stir, he finally feels the muscles in them at their full size, has one of those few moments in life where he knows how sexy and strong he really is. Grinning from ear to ear, he goes to grab his equipment.

∾

Yes, at this unfortunate moment I (Donna) am on the jailer's table, in his favorite room. It is a fairly frequent occurrence. "How does it feel when I do this?" he says, sticking something sharp into my shoulder blade until I scream.

I am afraid of my hands being broken. I am afraid of the bones being broken and never, never being able to help myself. Never being able to bring food to my mouth again. I am afraid he will maim my hands deliberately and I will be a husk of a person, just lying there in a corner waiting for the jailer to come and play with me yet more.

Why do I stay with him? WAIT, WHAT? Yeah, listen, Donna, this is important: WHY DON'T I JUST GET OFF THE TABLE AND LEAVE?

Silence. It's never occurred to me I could leave before.

Afterward, the jailer tells me,"You were wonderful." He gives me coffee and sugar buns.

It is a pleasure that he gives me these buns, the kind with glazing on top, because I am prediabetic and am not usually allowed to give myself them. If the jailer serves it to me it doesn't count. I try to drink the delicious coffee and eat the buns before dealing with him, but he grabs my head and makes me look at him. (I wonder, if I get diabetes, am I still going to return to this room?)

He says: "You were in terror just now and you can be there again."

∼

Today—yes, the same day as the torture session—I am not happy with everything my partner, E, does, and it makes me afraid that my love for her is a farce. Yes, part of me is actually worried about this, after 15 years together.

Would someone who really felt a lot of love be annoyed by her partner nervously going on about Trump when we're having dinner at a new friend's house? Be scared that her partner sounded awkward and unconfident? Look in her partner's face and wish that she were bold and bursting with self-love?

Why does E stir up the judge inside me? The jailer rants, in my head, about E's guarded chitchat. About something tactless she said to Fred.

The jailer wants to break our house to bits, kick down the beautiful floorboards and mix them with dog shit, with peed-on paper from the doghouse, smash in the windows, sledgehammer the mirrors, destroy the furniture we built together and the art we put on the walls and shatter glass until it is so dangerous in here I have to leave.

∼

The jailer resents E because she is imperfect, just as Donna is imperfect. Right now, he is hammering more sheets of lead onto the walls of the prison cells and her voice wafts over and he wants to take his hammer to E's lack of confidence and her absurd idea she's not pretty. He is worried she's not good for me. Wants to put E in the deepest, dirtiest, most toxic dungeon cell, the saddest, scariest one and he will take his hammer to her and wipe out, wipe out all of (both of our) awkwardness and self-hate.

∼

This reminds me of the time I was eight and thought my best friend Julie liked me only because I bought her bubblegum. She didn't have any money, and I had some and wanted to share. I really liked Julie, and we hung out all the time, but I was afraid she only liked me for my money.

Now I know Julie liked me for myself. But before the age of 12, I was certain that none of my friends liked me for me. I was sure they were with me only to get something from me. I often told them so and their feelings were hurt.

∼

As a teenager, I'd had a girlfriend who'd treated me badly and then dumped me, and my entire erotic self iced over for seven years. (Like someone under a hex.) I wanted a partner so badly, but no longer had the slightest idea how to get one. I couldn't even have a one-night stand. My sexual powers had left me, and I became like a female incel, starving all the time. Such a sterile season I found myself in, a land so dry, with nothing to help me but my mind.

I imagined a lover I could create myself, the way Zeus, maybe, develops Athena out of his head.

That way, maybe, I could ensure a partner who wouldn't hurt me.

In the more biological version of this fantasy, I would make a lover in my belly or my guts or my lungs and breathe it out of me. It—she—would emerge, slightly sticky, and love me.

In the more craft-based version, I would build her to my own specifications, like Pygmalion whittling out Galatea, making her exactly the right size to be my companion, my other, with curvy bits in all the right places, and exactly the kind of warm and honey-sounding voice I like.

She would be sexy and kind, and absolutely devoted to me.

∼

WHEW—I need a breather, shit!—Okay, pause, while I look at the cleaning schedule for the day. The cooking schedule, which I myself supervise and am quite good at. Yeah, also the panic-inducing work schedule. Let's take a little pause from this little pause to look at my relationship:

It's great. Er.

WHAT IF IT'S NOT GREAT WHAT IF IT'S NOT GREAT

Let's go back to walking Donnaville's streets: somehow in my mind's eye, I am never in the beautiful residential neighborhood or the place with the art buildings, I am in the garbage streets, the dangerous blocks. The wharf is always a fun place to go, with the sex workers and the poor kids. I'm not a exploitive pers— No, I reach out to something gentle and protective in myself instead.

Help me, I say to it. Please. I talk to it but not in words that the jailer might hear. I fervently think these words to it: Help me. From the center of the world (the center of myself?), something pulls me in, and I hug myself, embracing it.

CHAPTER 2

The divine mother—who has exactly that sort of warm and honey-sounding voice herself, as it turns out—watches with a guilty shock and horror as the jailer hurts them. Hurts Khachiya, Glenn, Leslie, Sloppy, Nehemiah, and Donna. Now that her song is finally getting through Donna's barriers, Magna can see inside the prison, although its unbreakable magic wards against her do not allow her to enter the inmates' cells.

She has fretted for years about what all might be going on down there in Donnaville. But what with one thing or another—revolutionary new methods of love and sex to attempt, exotic new varieties of compassion to sample, new strains of cannabis to grow—the divine mother simply hasn't hit on any ways of protecting Donna's people till now other than attempting to sing to them.

Now, though, the goddess must take action. She flies down to Donnaville straight to the little door outside the jailer's cell.

The goddess is gigantically tall, and she must stoop to get inside, but she knocks tenderly on his door, which is ajar.

"Hello." Wow—the jailer has never heard such a beautiful sound as this lady's voice. A thrill goes through him. "Are you the jailer?" she asks him very softly.

The jailer is knocked for a loop. Kind women with beautiful voices aren't in the habit of seeking him out. "Yes," he says, putting on his extra-masculine, twice-more-deep-and-clear voice, which in fact is his true voice, though he speaks it only when he is being his best self. "Yes I am."

"I'm Magna," she says, smiling at him with compassion. "Would you like to give me a cup of tea?"

He stops himself from staring. No one ever just knocks on his door and asks for tea. In fact, in all the years he's lived here no one but his guards has ever knocked upon that terrible door.

"Come in," the jailer says, looking at her oddly.

She takes in the poorly lit, peeling-paint room, the iron bed, the cracked and leaden pitcher with a faint odor of sour milk. There is no chair, just a thick layer of dust on the floor. So she folds herself elegantly and sits on the dust on the floor.

"I'm very sorry I don't have any tea right here," says the jailer, who badly wants, for reasons even he can't understand, to be a good host. "But I'll go out and get you some."

∼

The jailer walks swiftly to a shopping district. People scuttle to get out of his way as he passes, shrinking and hugging the walls as he goes by.

He normally only goes outside to spy on people, or arrest them. Or fuck with them, in the case of the poor people by the fountain. Yell at them, whatever their station. The jailer has yelled at the most important people in the city and even, when he was really doing his job, whipped them with a cord in the public square. (He fondly remembers his speeches on those occasions: "It is more in sorrow than in anger. . . .")

For five decades, all he's needed to consume is milk. They

deliver it to his cell twice daily, in huge jugs, so he hardly ever needs to buy anything.

He comes upon a little old-fashioned grocery, V. Maedda Fancy Foods, with vegetables stacked in crates outside, broccoli, carrots, and fresh pea shoots. An attractive, reed-thin person, androgynous in a light green mantle, comes out and bows to him. "Mr. Jailer."

The reed-like person (is it possible their skin is actually light green?) beckons him inside, where it is cozy and dim.

"What's your best tea?"

"What tastes the best to you?" the shopkeeper asks warmly, looking into his eyes.

"Something delicious. Really good. Unusual. Like, if want to impress someone!"

The shopkeeper is strong and flexible as a vine, and they reach up and behind a high shelf to fetch him a small bundle. Their voice is like an alto recorder: "I think you'll really enjoy this one."

The jailer buys the smoky, rich-scented bundle along with 10 lumps of sugar and rushes back to his cell.

∼

A curious couple spot the jailer as he dashes by, an unhoused brother and sister near the fountain in the public square.

They pause the game of chess they have been playing with pieces of garbage, on a huge board they have rigged on the dirty grass by the fountain. And they watch the jailer steadily until he's out of sight.

The sister and brother often turn tricks with the tourists

(there are not that many ways of making a living in Donnaville). For years, the jailer's been singling them out for special treatment, both for obvious reasons and because the jailer's baton loves to come in contact with the man's bare thigh, dressed as it often is in boy panties.

Now his sister laughs maliciously. "So it's begun! I thought the goddess would never have the balls to do it."

He stares at her for a moment, fighting disbelief. Then he moves his queen into a square near the center of the enormous board they have jury-rigged on the grass. "Checkmate!" he cries, laughing uproariously.

∼

They are having tea. The jailer has surreptitiously borrowed two teacups and a kettle from CO Rathbaum who keeps them in his cubby for when he has night shift. The teacups have a blue flower design.

The jailer serves. "It is so nice to have you here, Ma'am."

The divine mother smiles, blushing a little. "I am so very happy to be here with you, Mr. Jailer." In fact she has always liked him, since he was just a speck in his mother's eye.

She thoughtfully examines the man's dark hair, his craggy brows, his power eyebrows. Then she looks into his nice, soft eyes.

She sips her tea—wow, that shit is good. "But you must have some other name than that."

The jailer looks embarrassed. "I have never known my real name."

"What did they call you when you were small?"

"They called me You Little Piece of Shit."

∼

The harlequin finally hooks up. It's very strange that it has taken him so long this time, when men all over Donnaville look at him wherever he goes. In midtown, the cute younger office workers with their suit jackets hooked over their arms, the 20-year-old stoners in the park with their little beard stubble, the brunette driving an ice cream truck, all stare, all make implicit offerings.

Right now, instead, the harlequin is getting fucked by an impassive-looking man eating franks 'n beans. The guy doesn't just look inattentive—he regards the harlequin with all the interest he might extend to a shower drain. Or maybe, a blender he was using to make himself a protein shake. As it happens, the man's lack of care and consideration arouses the harlequin to no end. The dude just doesn't give a crap if the harlequin gets any pleasure at all. Not just that, he obviously doesn't care if his big dick hurts him, so carelessly is he banging into him. Like I said, the harlequin freaking loves this. As the god of euphoria, he loves many different kinds of sexual arrangements, and this is definitely one of them! But at the same time, the man's apparent lack of respect and concern for him makes him, suddenly, so angry and sad that even the pleasure shooting up his anus makes him feel grumpy, disquieted. Well, this is new. He abruptly shakes the man off him. As the dude falls to the ground—WHAP! BAM! SPLAT!—the harlequin strides out the door of the turd's apartment.

∼

1979: I am 15 and raptly taking off my girlfriend Morgan's black Converse sneakers. They are filthy—they are always filthy, black on the white parts—and I lovingly take them off, remove her sweaty socks, and begin applying my mouth to her grubby feet. The toes are flecked with little black bits of dirt, and it is wonderful and terrible to kiss them, put my mouth down the length of the sole, and suck each toe and fetid bunion of my sacred 16-year-old mean, punk-rock goddess. Next, I will suck on her poisonous vagina, which will send its paralytic juices all through my body until I can't even stir from the floor.

∼

Scene: long ago.

The harlequin and the jailer are children together, living in a bone-dry house where the only other living beings are dust mites. A giant bag of cat food has been dragged down from a shelf and pounded by their children's fists until they made an opening, and the dry food has spilled all over the kitchen floor, which they scoop up desultorily.

The harlequin is seven, the jailer 11. The harlequin looks thoughtfully at the pellets in his hand and bravely drops them all into his mouth at once. He crunches on them with his teeth and starts to cry.

"I told you not to eat too many at once!"

"THIS IS TOO MUCH FOR US, WE HAVE TO GET AWAY FROM HERE," the harlequin screams. "THEY'LL BE BACK AT ANY MOMENT!"

The jailer puts his larger face right up against his brother's. "We're not going anywhere," he grunts, flecking spit onto his brother's cheek. "They'll find us."

The harlequin gets a determined look on his little face, and he marches toward their bedroom to collect some things, but the jailer, much bigger and stronger, smacks him on the head. "They'll hurt us," he says, and his young fists are already massive, the harlequin is falling in slow motion to the ground, an amazed look on his face, but before he hits the floor he turns invisible and flies out the window

∾

Meanwhile, the jailer and the divine mother have been having highly animated conversations over tea. The divine mother has just found out that the jailer always wanted to bake bread, but has never had access to an oven beyond the giant oven in which he sometimes burns prisoners.

"Wow, that's such a pity," the divine mother says. "But you would think we could find another oven for you somewhere in this whole city."

The jailer hesitates. He's not used to anyone saying anything this helpful.

Is she trying to make fun of him? He listens for a sneer in her voice.

Then, "It's true," he says. "I guess a lot of people would let me use their ovens if I asked them."

"You do have quite a bit of influence."

"I love bread," he says. "I've always wanted to make it, but nobody ever taught me."

∾

For her part, the divine mother has baked entire universes into existence. She has confected people, each with their own unique sugar-sprinkled topping and special flavors, and she has baked whole forests into existence on cookie sheets, sometimes using molds for the trees and sometimes shaping each individual tree by hand. All of the mountains emerged originally out of her oven, even the Himalayan range, and each of Saturn's rings was originally a layer of pastry.

(She works not just with dough and pastry, but with wood, marble, clay. At home in her workshop, she is surrounded by mallets and chisels, so she can build, build everything she imagines as each new lump of Being emerges from her hands: little houses, toys, ramps, a whole army of small animals that stalk things on the ramps and up and down her mountains and under the shade of tiny trees she also builds.)

"I like yeast breads especially," the jailer is telling her.

"How long since you've last eaten anything suitably yeasty?"

The divine mother is suddenly embarrassed by her own wheedling tone. She is ashamed of trying to seduce the man toward goodness like this, with delicious baking memories.

The jailer frowns. "Ages. When I was a boy, we sometimes went to my mother's coworker who baked. She had these sweet potato rolls, and something called a Kugelhopf, and a Bee Sting Cake that wasn't terribly sweet but had this layer of honey and almonds on top."

"How old are you, Jailer?"

He looks lost for a moment, and it takes her awhile to apprehend the look on his face.

"I don't know how old I am."

∽

An hour later, the harlequin is lying in his nut when he hears the strangest sound. Someone is knocking on his wall! It is a

Faraday cage, so nothing is supposed to be able to get in or out. But the technologists who invented Faraday cages were thinking of electromagnetic signals, not physical interventions like knocking.

The harlequin recovers his equanimity easily. He is, after all, smooth. "Who are you out there, darling?"

"It's me," the divine mother says sheepishly. "The divine mother. I just thought it might be nice to drop by and see how you're doing."

"Have we met?"

"A long time ago, pet. But you and I have communicated in dreams for just *ages*."

"Uh, nobody comes to my nut. How did you know it was here?"

"You're my golden-haired boy, hon," she says seriously, like a diner waitress. "My prince. I keep track of you."

The harlequin is disconcerted. He can't imagine ever having met this clingy goofy woman, this mommy, before. "I don't allow anyone to keep track of me. And no, we can't meet in here! This is a sacred place for me."

The divine mother smiles privately, inside her own head. "Why don't you come out here, then, and have a picnic with me?"

He wants to get rid of her, so he leaves the nut. He assumes she'll be overwhelmed by his beauty like everyone else, by his height and sweet hard muscles and blond blond hair like yellow flowers cascading.

He steps out of the nut, strutting.

She laughs behind her hand. The divine mother is even more beautiful than her son, and there is no pulchritude in the world that can faze her.

On the fly, she has created a little picnic table in the bit of woods that abuts the harlequin's black nut. "Here, I have an egg salad sandwich, a ham with pickles and mayo. Oh, and this nice meatball one with sauce."

He finds himself sniffing the air around her large paper bag, despite his best intentions. "I don't usually eat."

"I know! But you love food," she says, setting the food out gracefully on the ebony table she's created in the blink of an eye. "Look, deep purple grapes, your favorite."

He looks at her curiously. From her shopping bag, she's taken clusters of grapes even bigger than her hands. Gazing up at her suddenly, he sees what he hadn't before: She is *huge*. She towers over him. Disconcerted—has he ever met anyone taller than himself before?—he puts her firmly out of his mind.

Grapes are his symbol, and he hasn't eaten any in so long. He is the god of play, but he hasn't actually *played* in so long it worries him. He hasn't even had really good sex in . . . oh so long.

What has become of him?

On the table, she has set out three wrapped sandwiches along with the grapes, a thick wedge of cheese, and a small bottle of wine."

For you," she whispers. "Me, I can't drink anymore."

The harlequin feels stirred. Has it suddenly become spring, high on the mountain where he keeps his jewel? He feels something entirely mysterious and alive in the air around the picnic bench, in the trees that are still bare but reaching out hopefully into the mild air, on the whole mountain where the grass feels soft again under his naked feet.

She has set out a cut-glass tumbler in front of him. He pours and drinks.

∽

radiant sparks fly as I begin to walk
on the air, I walk in spherical
circles
I tumble over myself
as though I were perfectly
round
What's that?
[A sunflower appears and speaks to him (it is very tall):]
"Don't you ever want to get to know someone who is not you?"
Me-Harlequin: Yes! Of course I do.
[Sunflower:] "Well, you haven't acted like it."
I'm still tumbling, but I'm struck dumb, I feel sad. "What do I have to do?"
[Sunflower:] "Take a long walk."

CHAPTER 3

I live on the outskirts of our city, so I come walking in from the mountains to the lovely entertainment district where the ice cream shop is and the special fish taco store. The ice cream is creamy, I haven't had it in forever. The jailer has never gotten any, poor thing. Giacomo makes me one with strawberries and bits of hazelnut, I slurp at it and dreamily make eyes at the tourists. (I want a fish taco for later, too. I haven't been so hungry in as long as I can remember.)

There's a cute tourist dude in striped red seersucker pants and a little black watch cap, he walks a few feet ahead and looks back at me.

I beckon to the alley but he shakes his head and his little butt at the same time. "Let's go get an espresso," he says.

"Nah, I'm hungry," and I steer him into the fish taco joint, the smells coming from it have been making my mouth water even when I was still eating ice cream. The boy gets fried grouper and I get fresh lobster, I have no need of money once anyone looks at my face and I can buy out the store for us, I hook the two of us up with sparkling wine as well in paper cups.

"I haven't seen you around before," he says.

"I'm a homebody," I lie. His body smells sweet and acrid like the grouper.

"I'm with a tour from Upper Caspia, we live on the sea. I grew up on a red houseboat," and he has come forward to show me pictures, he wants to connect, fuck that shit for real but he just smells so damn good. Maybe I can crush the fish bits on him and squeeze a giant lime over his whole body? There are pickled onions, too, on the taco. I want to snatch a few and drop them on his head. STOP TALKING. Maybe I can just pour the Spanish bubbly over both of us?

"You don't seem very interested in this," and oh shit he's offended, oh no, he's getting up. "Oh please no, I just got distracted for a minute, tell me about your houseboat. Do you live on one now as well?"

And now he's showing me more pictures on his phone, he lives in a pink-orange boat with seven mates, must be a really stinko bathroom in there, gay men as punctilious housekeepers are way overhyped.

Oh no, now he wants to know about *my* living situation, I try to smile but all I want is to open those little stripey pants and shuck them from him like a peel from a banana. "Well, I live in this large nut. It's like a cool black sphere I guess, sort of hippie accommodations, but I know a lot of other places to go," and I try to grin my most radiant and even warmest grin at him, I can do warm.

OH NO! Now he really likes me, he looks at my eyes with his very brown ones, he is going to ask me to be his boyfriend next, he puts his arm around me and now I can smell the cologne with rum and cloves that they make down in Upper Caspia, "Let's go on a very long walk," he says he thinks winningly.

∼

Oh yes, I have always wanted to bake. Not just bread but cakes, things that could delight me and my mother, things that if you set them on the table could delight neighbors and all sorts of people you might meet, make them like me for once.

My mother's friend made this cake with honey-caramelized almonds on top, she served it to us with tea in a little china set. I haven't really made anyone tea before this lady now. That was so nice and it made me remember how I used to like women. So long ago, when I was quite young it was always my favorite pastime when my mother took me over to other women's houses so they could have coffee and I would play on the floor. I would look up at their legs under the table blushing bright, they seemed quite alive, and their conversation so vivid as well. Men didn't talk that way.

Magna is lovely, no one so nice has ever been in my rooms, it is sad to say. She's like a tall rose. I longed for women when I was younger, too, and of course I also pined for men, but I haven't longed for anyone in that way in so many years, other than those paler, barer itchings to cut into people or to make them wish they died before they ever came to me.

∾

We lie curled around one another like animals, it is strange that when people use "animals" as a metaphor they do not think about their loyalty. The lifelong bond of a wolf with another wolf or a goose with the goose she will never let go of.

Lying here with E, her big hand in my hair, on my back, and my head and shoulders on her chest, lying together in a whole I never want to leave, a sort of circle like two wolves in one den, clasped together in a mass of hair, teeth, paws and muzzle, never to be cloven.

∼

The jailer finds an oven to rent in a small commercial kitchen in the center of the city. At the goddess's suggestion, he showers off the gray smell of the dungeons each morning before he goes out to bake, and he dons a crazy purple outfit Magna gave him in lieu of his usual black burlap. "No one will ever recognize you in that," she told him, gifting him as well with a rose-heavy cologne to douse on his head before he sets out.

The outfit comes with a floppy purple Renaissance hat. The rest is a flowing blouse and pants in Pucci paisley, and it works. No one on the way over or at the commissary itself thinks he's the jailer.

In the giant kitchen there are people making suckling pig tacos, broccoli rabe, pot roast, and handheld apple pies. One lady has big batches of ragu and the jailer is surprised to find the smell appealing. He hasn't wanted food in lord knows when, but the sauce smells heady. He usually only consumes milk, so that ingesting is, for him, the same as being nauseated. But today, he doesn't want to feel disgusted, for some reason. He buys a big bowl of the ragu and sets it down at the only available station, where he has also put sugar, honey, raisins, almonds, eggs, lemons, oranges, flour, butter, cognac, a few sweet potatoes, and an enormous container of yeast.

He is almost never motivated by anything other than duty and duty's bizarre cousin, cruelty. But today, before he cooks, he first sits down on a tall stool by the counter and thoughtfully spoons the ragu. He dunks a hunk of one of the lady's rye baguettes in it. The jailer can taste chopped beef and pork, wine, tomato, onions, garlic, carrot, something . . . chopped-up sardines? and sausages.

All around the stainless steel stations, people are chopping greens, rubbing spices into hunks of meat, drinking coffee, shooting the shit. Ordinarily the small talk would bother the jailer, making him feel awkward and graceless. But today he sits unselfconsciously slurping the ragu while he listens with pleasure to the conversation falling around him like rain.

"The tourists are gonna hit at noon."

"None of them like cronuts anymore, just macarons. Trays and trays of macarons, so boring, all different colors."

"But the flavors are different," says the dealer who makes the handheld pies. "Espresso, coconut, ginger—they're really delicious different flavors."

The jailer imagines tasting new flavors every week—no, every hour. What would it be like to keep tasting supremely pleasurable different things like this, and actually swallow them after? To have them settle in his stomach, like this sustaining ragu, this bread?

At a break in the chatter, the jailer shyly ventures to speak. His tongue feels stiff and heavy. "I'm making Bee Sting Cake," he says, "Has, um, has any of you ever tried anything like that?"

∾

The harlequin is walking with the young man from Upper Caspia. The kid has brought the harlequin to the nicer part of the river, a good ways north of the dirty harbor. There, they walk the sandy, wooded shore in silence for a while. There are a lot of birds: hawks gliding, geese on the grass, surprisingly a white heron. There are gulls, a bird the harlequin is fond of because, like him, they are considered trashy. As one dives for an abandoned bit of pizza cheese, the harlequin reaches out his arm to the bird and the seagull perches happily on it, peering at the harlequin adoringly.

The kid, whose name is Hylas, smiles quizzically. "You sure have a way with wild animals."

The harlequin puts his other arm around Hylas and strokes his shoulder (the harlequin has a talent for caresses). "*All kinds* of wild animals," he says. His warm face makes a gesture like a smile and a hiss combined.

"You won't get sex off the brain, will you?"

"Never!" the blond god laughs.

He's surprised by how completely relaxed he is. He's been having a good time walking first the daffodil-laden residential streets and then the greenway and the river with young Hylas, and he doesn't even feel annoyed or frustrated or overwhelmed as he always does with boys who don't want to have sex right away. Hylas has that twangy Caspian accent, and he's loose and sweet and fun and keeps saying interesting goofy things about the houseboat counterculture In Upper Caspia, which is full of crafters and anarchists.

"On the boats," Hylas says, "no one is ever prosecuted for weed, and everyone exchanges, like, art they just made and sourdough starters and cupcakes all day long."

"I'd like to go there." The harlequin has been feeling strangely parochial today, like a juror who has been sequestered for generations. The problem with being the most sophisticated person in your town is you can forget just how much you have never learned or seen.

"I'll take you there, Bobby," says the young man earnestly, looking deep into his eyes.

The harlequin has told Hylas that his name is Bobby. Now the harlequin is starting to regret this lie, but he has never told one person his real name and he's not about to start now.

"Didn't your parents know your real name?" Donna interrupts into his thoughts.

The harlequin is peeved. *Get outta my head. I'm just trying to enjoy myself.* He wants to focus on Hylas's sunny voice and on his calves sticking out of the seersucker Capris.

"Who says I have parents?" he thrusts the words in Donna's face, making a rude gesture with his teeth, and stalks off, following Hylas down the grass.

∼

Anna, the butch young woman who makes the handheld apple pies, comes over to the jailer's station to show him how to use the electric hand mixer. He'd borrowed it from the common shelf and started mixing the batter for his Bee Sting Cake, but as soon as he turned the thing up to the required speed, batter flew out all over unto his hair, the counter, and his eyebrows.

"You have to put a paper plate over the mixing attachments for the batter not to fly out, if you run it on that speed," she tells him.

"Why? None of the recipes mentioned anything like that."

"In baking, you can't rely on what they say to do," Anna says, handing him a hot little pie. "Recipes are wrong all the time." He grumbles to himself, perturbed, surprised. Sinks a tooth into the juicy thing, mutters thanks.

∼

The previous afternoon:

The child can hear the goddess's song, but only partially. It's like hearing something underwater—it feels like miles of rushing ocean are pressing their salty unintelligibility hard against her ears. Before, she couldn't hear anything of the divine mother's voice, but now it's like a distant sweet sound (she can't make out the words) muffled by a heavy blanket. Moreover, something inside her keeps erupting in scary, high-pitched feedback.

Then the jailer comes in and kicks her in the kidneys.

"You fucking little bitch," he says. "You miserable little piece of shit."

What difference does it make that she can hear a nice sound in the back of her head, every couple of hours?

∽

Finally alone, the divine mother rests after her long day, rubbing oil on her cheeks and neck, eating some marijuana tincture and five fudgy brownies while she watches the robins cock their heads boldly for worms in her backyard.

"Mommy!" they cry, overjoyed to see her, "Mommy!" and they hop closer to her, still scanning the soil for movement. She wishes she had made the birds' breasts lipstick-red instead of orange, they are duller than she intended. "Hi, little cuties!" she says, stroking their tailfeathers.

The doodies from her composting toilet gaze at her with love, missing the warmth of her body already. She regrets that they have to leave her body and go on their own.

∽

Next morning, the divine mother takes a Pilates class. But she just can't figure out what the teacher wants her to do. If she puts her left knee in front, how can she possibly put her right leg behind her at that angle? She feels like a clumsy idiot.

Yet she knows she is not a clumsy idiot. The spark of the divine presence within her tells her she does not need to perfectly intuit at all times how the Pilates teacher thinks she should arrange her knees and legs. It tells her she is perfect already.

When class is over, she determinedly puts bright candy-red lipstick on in the bathroom, because she has a hot date with herself later that afternoon.

∼

E holds me in her huge hands and reels me into her so she can see my face more closely. The eyes in the enormous head gaze at me tenderly as she strokes me carefully, delicately, impossibly with those enormous hands, so that I feel like a small person in love with the giant Lord or Lady of the Lake. A small person loved by a giant personage who surrounds me and romantically dances with me and fulfills me, oh fulfills me, oh fulfills me.

How can those hands enter, again and again, the smallest parts of me? How can they possibly avoid hurting me? Yet they never ever hurt me, it is a mystery of the sacred divine.

∼

It's time for the jailer to go back and check on his prisoners, and he's feeling curiously panicky.

~

I often feel that I have to obey anyone who wants me to do anything. I feel like I have to obey even unspoken commands, intuited from the ether. I don't WANT to do the thing some other person wants me to—make a salad, go to some event with them, put the coffee on. But I do it anyway, feeling defeated, crushed. Battered, not a person, I do the thing, feeling like an automaton, and often find out later that the person didn't even actually want me to do that particular thing anyway.

~

The jailer arrives at the hidden warren of prison cells at the center of town. He feels leaden. There are six prisoners "in" today, and as always, quite a lot of disgusting filth to clean up: human waste, the gamy stench of piss like in a monkey house, dust full of tears. Sometimes it is the stench that frightens new prisoners the most.

(It frightens him too. It frightens him too. It frightens him too. He imagines lying in his own filth and not being cared for—not being allowed to be cleaned up from it. He imagines, as he goes inside, being hit with his own officers' truncheons. Not being able to stop himself from screaming uncontrollably.)

~

All my life, I've been dreaming of piss and shit, sad dreams where I walk around looking for a place to pee but every toilet is horribly dirtied and full. Even in the enormous public bathrooms of my dreams, or in offices incomprehensibly full of toilets, toilets not even separated by stalls, toilets out in the middle of everyone's desks and chairs, or part of dowdy feminine gyms and spas, mysteriously threaded in among the exercise machines, every fixture is already overfull and soiled. Deliberately, unbearably soiled and full.

~

The jailer approaches his chief deputy, CO Gray, for the duty roster. Gray is a handsome fiftyish little man in a sharp gray uniform in which he looks like Darth Vader's lieutenant. He salutes the jailer mockingly and puts a heavy clipboard in his hands.

The roster reads: "Jailer: Mop, bleach, vacuum, torture prisoners." The jailer feels much too tired to deal with any of these, but he decides to torture the prisoners as it is the least insufferable of his many insufferable duties. He decides to get coffee first.

"Gray! Who is it who requires dolor this morning?"

"Sir! Leslie. Nehemiah. Glenn. Khachiya. Sloppy. Or we could just do you!" He snickers.

The jailer sighs and creeps up a back passageway to the officers' dingy little break room. Three guards, lounging at the linoleum table, are stunned that he has had the audacity to enter their special room.

"Yo Jailer boy!" says CO Smith patronizingly. "What do you need?"

"Coffee," the jailer says, almost to himself, smiling crookedly. He has never dared to use their coffeemaker before. The guards stand up pointedly and wait for him to leave, arms crossed. After he pours himself a cup, he conspicuously dumps the rest out in the trash and wipes his hands on the knifelike creases of the pants of CO Gray, who has just entered the room.

∼

Leslie is waiting in a dim room with brown-red walls and a musty scent coming from both her and the walls and floor. When he walks in, he has the sudden feeling that he is about to cut into himself. He imagines a large watermelon he has to cut, or a freakish honeydew. At first he can't make himself do it, but after a moment he steels himself and grabs a scalpel from a hook near the door.

∼

The harlequin is giving writing lessons to Donna.

Sharp bursts, he is saying. Intense.

Make it as alive as possible. He is trying to get her to understand.

You need the juice. Without it, there is nothing.

"I love juice," she says thoughtfully.

Pluck out your eye if it's not working. Make sure everything is either seething or cold as bone.

Pluck out the fucking weeds by the roots and plant me there!

∼

"I'm going to hurt you," he says, stroking the place on her side where her waist curves. Leslie's smell is sharp in the little room and he feels giddy. There is a black, buckled wonderful leather bag over her head and he remembers that day 30 years ago when she did not appear interested in going for a soda with him and he remembers his shame-filled rage, how he wanted to throw her down a flight of stairs and see her broken body at the bottom. See her weeping realizing her bones jutted out from her skin and her legs were no longer able to walk.

Now he is leaning above her and she has not been able to wash her body in eight months and he takes off her bag to smack her head and watch the blood fall in her eyes.

"I remember you," Leslie whispers. "Poor thing."

∽

Horrified and wanting her to JUST. STOP. TALKING. He's taken the scalpel from its hook when Leslie, who has turned on her side toward the wall, says, "It's funny, I couldn't figure out what you were going on about that day when you kept mentioning Dr Pepper, I just wish you had been able to tell me that you wanted a date."

He's embarrassed to hear this, even more embarrassed than he usually is, and so he stands there coated in shame and fumbling with his bag of toys, trying to figure out how to free her from his jail, when Leslie grabs the scalpel from him and plunges it firmly into her own chest. She's been waiting for this chance for decades—her one chance at freedom from horror, forever.

Before the jailer can emerge from his shame fog long enough to pull the scalpel out of her, she's gone.

∽

The harlequin is drinking a beer. Hylas is off with his fellow queens from Upper Caspia, checking out the city's boring nightlife. The harlequin misses him already, but he's been itchy for a break from all the togetherness, it makes him afraid he will lose his edge. Is pleased to feel like his lone, shady self again, perching on his heels on a nice low white fence outside the touristy gay pizza place.

He watches queer boys and women and the young enby folk frolicking, rolling their tongues around the tips of the pizza where the cheese hangs off. He gets invisible to join them, biting the cheese off with them and mingling in their Budweiser caresses. Now he's stroking a lovely long-haired boy, he loves long hair SO MUCH and he is touching the chestnut locks but the boy thinks it's just the wind.

So many myths about the wind being sexual with people, the harlequin remarks to himself dreamily. There is Boreas, Zephyr, Enlil. (He loves all stories.) The wind-gods touching every woman they want reminds him of the old days in Italy, when he would tie the horses' manes and sometimes women's hair in knots for fun, his mischievous, rude, and taunting side that folks don't always like. He's been known to spoil cream when he doesn't get what he wants.

The harlequin doesn't believe in boundaries, at least not for other people. He is afraid of ending up in a nonsexual wasteland, nothing but comfort and warmth as far as the eye can see but no ecstasy, nothing sacred and burning. If he's not burnt he can't fulfill his function.

∽

Trying to keep from passing out, the jailer backs out of Leslie's room and darts into the chamber holding Glenn. Glenn has only been taken recently and he is tall, pale, and won't shut up. "Neoliberal," he is hissing, "elite," and he actually springs from the table to spit lavishly in the jailer's face. The jailer is quietly delighted by this and masters himself more than usual so he can shock Glenn when he applies a nutcracker to Glenn's swollen left testicle.

∼

The harlequin is sick of eating pizza and pretending to be the wind. Being invisible is no fun after a while, and the boy with gorgeous hair is boring, going on and on to no one in particular about Andrew Yang.

But what else can the harlequin do? If he goes to the bars he might run into Hylas.

∼

The following morning, the jailer sets out to bake. He's excited about yeast rolls. Maybe the cute butch girl will want one. The divine mother contrives to run into him along the way, appearing halfway along the route to the commercial kitchen. She holds out a glass pitcher in an odd rhombus shape, with some beer she just brewed.

"Mr. Jailer! I have a little gift for you."

He looks up at her, as he always does, with a shock of joy. It's a hot day, and as she pours some fizzy beer for him in a diamond-shaped glass, he drinks it with a sense of overweening goodness and pleasure and well-being that would be impossible for literally anyone to deserve, and drinks it down.

∼

The harlequin goes home, dejected. Hylas never even came to look for him after the bars closed. He slinks to his nut, buttoning all the hatches, creeps inside. Theoretically, he believes masturbation is just as wonderful as sex with any partner. But secretly, he would be shamed and depressed to have to masturbate rather than being with someone glorious.

(From afar, the divine mother looks at him fondly, bemusedly, with pity. She loves masturbation and would never be embarrassed about it.)

He stretches out in the four infinite directions of his nut and feels, for the first time, lonely.

∼

People sniff loudly as the jailer comes into the great kitchen, for he forgot to shower this morning and he still smells of agony and rot, from the work with Leslie and Glenn. The divine mother breathed in his smell earlier when they met, and had to immediately supply one of her own vast breaths of clean air from the core of her being so as not to sob.

The woman who makes the ragu—her name is Conchetta—wordlessly puts up a plastic sheet around her kitchen space so it doesn't affect her meat mixture as she chops. Anna of the handheld pies wonders if the jailer has turned homeless or if some drug has, after weeks, made him lose all hope of self-care.

All the other cooks and bakers are now guarding their stations and hoping the jailer doesn't get near their macarons or white almond mole. The jailer doesn't know what's up, although he notices people are looking at him funny, like they used to back in school. He sets up his own station, ignoring them and loving the stainless steel, the ferociously scrubbed and glistening oven, even the bins of flour and spices that have been kept completely free of dust and gnats by the female geniuses the kitchen hires nightly.

He washes his hands and starts mixing flour, butter, and milk, when Anna strides over to him.

"Dude! You stink."

"M-me? I stink?" the jailer responds as if paralyzed.

"You smell *bad*. Like, you rolled in shit. No offense, dude, but it's hard to make food here when you smell like that."

He's still frozen as ever, but it gradually dawns on him that Magna must have known what she was talking about when she insisted that he wash the jailhouse off himself each morning before cooking. He thought she was just recommending it as a sort of New Age-y self-nurturing thingy, like meditation or ritual walking.

He smells himself thoughtfully. He can't detect anything different from the normal scent of his life, but he yelps, "Thanks, young lady" and ducks into the cooks' large washroom at the back, which has two showers.

～

In the mirror, his naked body is hairy and potbellied, but his face is small and nebbishy. Few people have ever told him he is beautiful, and he has never found himself to be.

The soap in the cooks' shower smells like jasmine. He washes himself with it gently. His body is pale, but it could look like a flower I suppose to someone who thought fondly of me, he thinks idly. His nipples are tiny and a bit too pink. His penis looks like a little apostrophe, or a mistake.

He washes the gray flower of his body and thinks back to a time when he was even so bold as to offer it to someone. Or when someone, a few someones, were even so audacious as to accept.

∽

The harlequin wakes up feeling more depressed than ever. His mouth tastes like something has been burnt inside, and when he goes to the magnificent outdoor bathroom he's installed in the next clearing, he is shocked to find himself looking unbeautiful in the mirror.

His face has the first wrinkles he has ever detected. His hair looks straggly and split-ended. His nose and cheeks are threaded with purple veins.

What the fuck is this?

Even his beautiful sixpack has a little fat roll hanging off it.

What is more, there is a pink-green rash with a bad scent on his penis.

His toes look crooked. Is that fungus on his little toe?

He rushes toward the stream that runs through the rill because, suddenly, he must drink what feels like living water. He cups his hands and drinks.

CHAPTER 4

After the harlequin has slurped the water he straightens slowly and walks a few feet under the trees. What would it mean to become someone other than the person he has always been?

It would be hard. He has always been young and strong.

He has always been full of power. It springs from his chin in little tufts, and from his head in bouncy ringlets.

No one has ever been able to conquer him.

No one has ever been able to make him suffer. (He is lying his head off, as always. Long ago he did suffer, but he has grown so much in gorgeous unassailable power he forgot it long ago.)

Gods are timeless. Now the harlequin has entered time.

∼

The jailer washes his clothes in the sink, then puts them on his now-clean body. He moves his fingers through his dark, oily, wavy hair to comb it.

He secretly thinks his bushy eyebrows are kind of cute. They make him look like Bert from Bert and Ernie.

He returns to the gigantic kitchen space, blazing into the bare room in his Pucci paisley, and everyone looks up but this time their noses are untroubled.

He smiles a very open smile, as though his head had been

cracked open but somehow it was liberating and didn't hurt him. And starts separating eggs at the counter.

∼

The harlequin starts walking into town. He is hungry, although until that unsightly old lady came with the sandwiches the other day, he had never actually *needed* to eat. The change might be disconcerting, if food didn't taste so good.

He walks down Sandy Bottom Road and Red Brush Road, turns left by the birch tree, and skips a little as he gets to the rock where the real walk begins down to the inns and attractions.

He had a bad morning, it is true, but nothing beats a walk in the cool sunshine down a wooded road. Whistling, he hops down the road and, turning around a bend, comes face to face with Hylas.

∼

"Were you really not planning to spend any more time with me before I leave?" Hylas says in a teasing tone, setting his index finger on the harlequin's breastbone.

The harlequin—I don't know his real name yet, so let's just call him Bobby—feels his face open up with delight, its corners stretched so far by a smile it can't possibly get any wider.

"I wanted to," Bobby says, and he takes Hylas's hand. They walk together into Old Town and arrive at the fanciest little restaurant there, which is open for midmorning breakfast.

At the counter Bobby orders them fig focaccia with chêvre and very strong coffee spiced with chicory. Hylas gets them a table by a corner window. Warm sunlight is flooding in, somewhat milky, and the waitress brings them a salad of edible flowers on the house.

∽

The divine mother steps into her workshop with a pot of coffee and a basket of sour cream blueberry coffeecake. Today she is planning to sculpt things out of mud, coffee grounds, ripe bananas, and bits of flowers and berries.

She has nice dark brown wet mud assembled at her feet, and a giant bucket of coffee grounds. Now, one by one, bananas emerge out of the air for her, shuck off their peels, and settle in her hands.

Magna mushes them up with the mud and the coffee, then delicately, with a small tweezer, adds pieces of roses, violets, bluets, purple tulips, and stargazer lilies to the mush. Finally, from a giant bowl, she pours mulberries, raspberries, and dancing golden cloudberries, which take over everything by forming the mud-banana-coffee-flower mixture into clothing for themselves, cute shorts with little suspenders and flaring wide skirts, and start a conga line dancing on Magna's shoulders before she can even sculpt anything out of the mess.

∽

A raven flies in but doesn't peck at the food. "You forgot to teach the jailer baking," it says. "You set him up in a kitchen and you forgot to teach him any actual baking."

"Doody! Fuckballs! Ass tripe!" the divine mother curses cheerfully. "I knew there was something I forgot to do!"

∼

The child feels somehow more awake than she can remember. She is stirred, as though a light breeze had entered the uninvadable walls of her cell, as though trees were growing there whose naked branches it could stir. As though there were even a crocus, poking up through the filthy straw. Of course there are no flowers, no trees—this is still her freezing/scorching cell with its stink that would devastate everyone but the jailer and the child. They are both used to it. There are several messes on the floor. But the girl feels, somehow, more alert and more watchful, strangely more alive.

∼

Anna asks if the jailer would like to go for a drink after work, which for the two of them usually ends at 2 PM. He is mortified, because he hasn't socialized with anyone for decades.

Though it's true the jailer sometimes fills in as husband to E, he can't exactly call that socializing. It's more that he supports her with as much warmth and heroism as he can muster, which, from the warmth point of view, is considerably more than you might imagine.

When he attempts to answer Anna he moves very slowly, like a skeleton coming to life. His voice sounds disused. But in his creaky, halting way he can distinctly be heard to say, "Ah . . . thank you. I would enjoy that very much."

She takes him to a grungy all-gender queer bar, but it turns out the loud, garbage-filled, graffiti-decked place is run by a wine enthusiast. Everybody else is drinking beer, but the jailer orders them a bottle of rare 30-year-old Haut-Bergey, Pessac-Leognan and Anna bows over her hands at him and grins. (She is both handsome and pretty, the kind of butch with slightly curly dark hair, cut short but not that short, and slightly curvy, with shiny jewelry and studs glinting at her wrists, neck, and waist.)

The wine, it turns out, is very complex and balanced and beautiful, and Anna starts talking to him about her life.

∽

"I came to Donnaville to skateboard back in '77, but eventually I ditched it all for lyrical baking. As much sensuality and emotion as I could cram into a piece of pastry," she says. "It turned out this place was good for that. Like creating a poem, but for your mouth," she adds as an afterthought.

The jailer says, "The kind of writing I like best is stirring, but political."

Anna isn't quite sure what to say to this riposte. "I never really thought about the art of political writing."

"Oh, it is an art," says the jailer, who is so sensitive on the subject that some have had their fingernails torn out for merely arguing the point. "People think all beautiful writing is fancy stuff about nothing. They are wrong," and he abruptly picks his ear.

"Tell me what you like best about beautiful political writing," Anna says.

"It can influence people. It has all your heart in it. And the sentences are rolling!" This is more than the jailer has said to anyone in years.

"So, what are your politics like?"

"I am anti-violence and pro-socialism," he says proudly. "The government must care for everyone."

∼

Hylas and Bobby have just entered Hylas's guesthouse, a sweet gay place with dried flowers and cheerful old paintings, and proceeded quickly to Hylas's room on the second floor. The door is painted Persian blue and when Hylas unlocks it they almost fall inside. Bobby puts his hand on Hylas's cheek and roughly/delicately guides him to the bed. Hylas then seizes him and turns him on his back, so Hylas can lie athwart his hips and kiss him, while their legs twine firmly around each other.

Bobby scrabbles at the other boy's clothes and tears open the other's shirt to reveal the radiance of his chest, a message so stunning he must pause for a few seconds to take in its magnanimity. Bobby is all about beauty, but the beauty of the *other*.... The beauty of the *other* ... surprisingly ... takes him to a place he did not think he could ever get to, a place beyond desire and into fulfillment and ease.

With his whole hand, he touches Hylas's face so softly he surprises himself.

∼

"Well, I like your politics," Anna says. "But you're fairly new to baking, right? What's your other job?"

The jailer turns dark red and mumbles into his shirt collar.

"What's that? I didn't quite get that."

Mumble bumble fog.

"What?"

"I'm in law enforcement," the jailer says finally, enunciating perfectly. For some reason Anna cannot comprehend, he looks furious.

～

"Huh, what kind of law enforcement?" Anna asks.

"Nothing very impressive," he murmurs. The jailer appears to fold and shrink into himself even more than usual, to become dry and wispy as though he were small apple slices in an oven.

"Dude. I'm not a great fan of law enforcement, but you seem to me like the kind of person who's probably pretty impressive at what you do. You should stop putting yourself down."

"There are some things I'm good at," he admits. A look of fear passes over his face.

～

When the harlequin wakes up, it is dim in the little room and the birds are singing feebly. He looks at Hylas lying there, so innocent in sleep, beautiful closed eyelids nestled around a dream. He is horrified suddenly. Oh fuck, fuck no.

I feel like a murderer. Because I'm going to hurt him, there's no question. I'm going to hurt this man. And Hylas, who makes himself so vulnerable, Hylas with his little-boy features, is the perfect mug, the perfect one for me to love and abandon. I who have abandoned so many.

But I have no choice! I never did. I haven't slipped out of jail cells all my life just to be caught now at the finish line.

～

After Anna and the jailer leave the bar, it's long past time for the jailer to report to his real job. His ankles feel so heavy it's like lifting a bowling ball. He imagines them pierced through and connected by an iron chain. But who is it who controls that chain? Is it simply all the wine he drank with Anna that's making him come to a dead stop every couple of feet? Or is he—*am I, he wonders*—for once acknowledging what he is doing, reverting ever closer to the invisible center of pain?

Why does he keep returning?

He can feel all the pain in the prison. Has always felt it—felt it decades before he became its warden.

Even as a child he felt it. The wretched chambers at the center of this land, the invisible prison at the heart of this world, draw him horribly, inevitably, although he hates them, although—

NO. He forces himself to sit down on the curb for a minute, breathing heavily. Factory trucks, garbage trucks, refrigerator trucks, mortuary trucks pass him by. Suddenly he is ravenous—he hasn't eaten anything since he chugged some milk last night. But he can't abide the thought of milk right now without retching. He hates the sustenance he assigned himself so long ago—when he'd decided that in a terrible world, he needed to be an example of discipline at every moment, an example of rectitude and commitment.

He doesn't want to go back. HE ALWAYS GOES BACK. It is his only real virtue.

The only good thing about him is his constancy. He can suffer forever, and make others suffer.

∼

Bobby sprints out of the room. He is good at passing undetected, good at getting out while someone is sleeping or not noticing or not realizing yet what he is. Moving extraordinarily quietly, lighter on his feet than anyone else in this ridiculously loud and heavy town, he ducks his head and moves around the corners, running into none of the gay guests or staff or the lone woman he can hear in the front room polishing and dusting everything. He moonwalks into the breakfast room to grab a glazed donut and is out the front door before you can say Jack Robinson.

∽

Hylas wakes up in the guesthouse.

∽

The jailer has been sitting on the curb for about 40 minutes, grinding his teeth. Suddenly he gets up and starts walking in the direction he came from—back toward the commercial kitchen. He doesn't know what he's going to do when he gets there, but he knows he can't return to the prison again today. Maybe tomorrow, but not today. He knows that he won't be able to keep holding the fat old blowtorch as it burns Khachiya, Glenn, and Sloppy, even though he hates Khachiya and Glenn.

He skitters through Donnaville's abandoned factory section, keeping his head down so none of his boys out on patrol will see him. He makes his silhouette thin and scoots into a little restaurant. Once inside, he lets out a breath and orders empanadas.

The chef comes out, an enormous person in whites. "Hey! Aren't you the new station at the kitchen? You're making something with honey."

"Yesss . . . a Bee Sting Cake. An old family friend used to make it."

"But you're kind of green, aren't you, buddy?"

"Green?"

"You haven't cooked professionally before." The chef looks apologetic as he says this.

"No, it's true, I can't really cook," the jailer says. "I can barely eat."

∼

He looks cadaverous sitting there, like Nosferatu in the silent movie. The jailer loses his potbelly at times of great stress, and many who saw him just before they lost consciousness have said he had the look of a buzzard. A curious thing about the warden of Donnaville is that his size is not fixed. He can be fat and strong at night and a bag of bones the next morning, for he shrinks and grows in relation to Donna's need.

The empanada chef is a little freaked out by the look of the jailer, it's true. But he's also liked the guy since he first encountered him, trying earnestly to figure out which bowls to use and whether or not to work with pre-sifted flour. The chef brings out a platter of golden half-moons and sets them in front of the skeleton.

"This is something new I'm working on," he winks, "*mpanatigghi*, almond-ground beef-lemon-chocolate empanadas from Italy."

The jailer is starving, and these things are delicious.

∼

The harlequin is hiding in a haystack at a horse-riding theme park in the entertainment district. He dived under the hay because he's shaking. Usually it's fine when he leaves boys, but what he felt in that room—a vastness, a starry space really—was different from the kinds of bigness or brightness he had felt before when having sex. What he felt was not so much that he was being carried out of the course of ordinary events, as that he was going *deeper into them*.

Normally, sex is holy for him because it is the ultimate breaking of the locks. The thing that makes him know in his bones he is free and comes from fire. But the connection with Hylas in that room didn't feel like a divine escape as much as an ingress, a coming towards, deeper into, a tasting and enjoying of what is.

He doesn't know how he feels about that.

He doesn't know how he feels about the whole business of "going in" or "enjoying what is." Isn't the ordinary world stupid, corrupt? Is it bourgeois to enjoy what is?

Clasped around Hylas like that, he felt like a predator.

Is it okay to be a predator?

∼

The jailer is creeping through the streets, almost crawling, as the stars peep out and the shadiest characters of Donnaville emerge from their hidey-holes. CO Gray flits around a corner and a couple of vampires in flashy clothes walk without touching the ground down 86th Street, pausing to work in a game of dominoes with CO Smith.

The jailer wonders where Anna goes this time of night.

Does she have a night job? Is she seeing someone? He knows better than to expect romance with her—but does she think he's a nice person? Is she glad she thought of him for a friend? And is her job, or whatever it is, safe to walk to?

But why would anybody want to be his friend?

∼

Magna hitches her two llamas, Sensuality and Delight, to her gleaming red wagon and drives downtown. She parks them in front of the empanaderia and peers around the corner at the jailer, concerned.

∼

The jailer edges close to the buildings so he won't be seen. People are so often afraid of him that he hasn't been in active fear for years, except for those few moments every day when he arrives at work—when he can see himself, taste himself, smell himself in his victims' place.

Now he tries to model his own bravado from the prison best as he can and stands, looking sardonic and tough, against the side of a closed-up store that sells cheap clothes. He wishes he had his old cap from back in the day, his old jeans and tough-guy shirt, it would make him feel a little more protected than his dirty floppy purple Renaissance hat and flowing effeminate blouse.

∼

The harlequin hasn't left his haystack, even when the horse theme-park actually closed for the night and he realized, weeping, that he, the most beautiful god in the world, had taken on the smell of the fleet animals and their droppings.

He feels even more wretched, if that is possible, but finally, after three hours, he forces himself to rise up from the smelly hay and look around at the horses. An insane number of these animals are kept available so that Donnaville's large tourist population can meander and sightsee from the back of a 1000-pound force of nature.

A black gelding draws up to him from a stall that has been left unlocked. The beast juts his nose into the harlequin's hands. Bobby breathes in his scent sharply. His hide is calming to the touch, and Bobby cannot believe the warm, jaunty look on the gelding's face. The animal reminds him of himself. Still feeling terrible, but comforted as he is always able to be comforted, the harlequin laughs softly and jumps on the gelding's back and rides it out the door.

∽

The jailer decides to jimmy open a car in a dimly-lit downtown parking lot and sleep inside. Actually, it is more comfortable than his iron bed at home. He falls asleep so quickly on the leather seats that he wakes up feeling more refreshed than in years.

∽

The sister and brother by the public fountain have started to spread the word that something's wrong with the jailer. He didn't come in last night and many in the city's large population of indigents and petty thieves have found this news most interesting.

Sister: "He's been working in there every day for 50 years, nobody just decides they don't feel like sticking knives in people anymore and want to go to Aruba."

Brother: "Maybe he keeled over."

A thief: "Maybe they finally tossed him and he'll turn up in the charity food distribution next week, he'll be the one that smells like fish."

Sister: "I hope they tossed him. He's already in the stomachs of 10 rats. Give those rats a high-five for me as they go by!"

∼

In the night-time:

The harlequin has ridden through all of Donnaville on the gelding, who he has named Falhófnir after one of the horses ridden by the Norse gods. But when Bobby starts to reverse directions and gallop Falhófnir back through the city again at half-lightspeed—as he's still able to do—he suddenly begs the horse to stop so abruptly, in such a weird whispery scream, that Falhófnir looks at him curiously, pulls up and pees in a sudden copious steaming shower. The harlequin jumps down to the curb and sobs. Falhófnir bends his head down to the man, reaches out a foreleg as though it were a hand, and comforts him.

∼

The jailer hears a soft knock on his car window. When he looks up it is Magna, all 8 feet of her, beaming down at him as she rocks a candy red dress. He has wanted to see her more than anything, but he's stabbed with shame.

It is early morning. He wants to crush himself into the back-seat floor so she can't see his face. But he rolls down his window.

"I abandoned my post," he says. "I'm not worthy of having you look at me," and he curls up like a dying bug.

Magna laughs, and it sounds like silver, as she reaches out two fingertips and touches his face. "Don't be silly, my boy," and it is the softest touch he has ever known, how can it be softer than the most delicate down feathers, than the pocket cloth they give the Queen that he once felt at a very great cost, how?

She kisses his brow. "I bet you need a shower," she says, "and some new clothes." And indeed, his floppy purple ensemble has become very ripe and humid from the night downtown. She draws with her index finger in the air atop the car and a large blue-silver airy rectangle appears, a little wider than the Lexus he picked out to sleep in. Inside the blue-silver room of air appear a gleaming shower and bathroom, private, in white marble, and on a low wood table are his new raiment, sleek and black, pants and sexy-buttoning shirt, and at the top of the pile is a motorcycle cap.

∼

Bobby wakes in a pool of horse-piss and human vomit, but the horse is there to nudge him out of the mess and insist he mount Falhófnir and ride to the coffee bar. With the horse waiting on the patio, Bobby goes in the bathroom and gets cleaned up, but when he orders chocolate-sea salt granola and a macchiato for himself plus rolled oats for Falhófnir he's surprised to see the counterperson look at him expectantly.

"Did you need something from me?" asks Bobby in his usual tone of polite imperiousness.

"That'll be $11," the barista says firmly.

Consternation. In the over 50 years the harlequin has been alive (for he is much older than he looks) no one has ever asked him to pay for anything. His face, his litheness is currency enough. He staggers for a moment. "Sorry," he says. He has no money.

The barista takes pity on him and lets him have the macchiato, already pulled, for free.

∼

The jailer, marveling, showers in the glorious bathroom, where sparkly lines of gold are striated through the marble and the divine mother has thoughtfully left Royall Bay Rhum cologne, his favorite from 30 years ago, on the wash stand.

∼

He has to feed Falhófnir, so the harlequin decides to busk. He improvises an instrument out of Falhófnir's leather saddle, drumming on it as he sings in his glorious rockstar tenor. An 11-year-old boy comes up to tell him, "You're a really good singer," and a couple of tourists point him out to each other and look highly interested. But by the end of three hours, he's only made $2.25.

He takes it to the barista. The latter makes some thoughtful calculations in his head, reaches into a side cabinet, and comes out with half a portion of oats in a plastic bowl.

∾

"You look handsome," the divine mother says. The jailer feels perplexed and angry. Is she trying to play a trick on him? He feels a familiar confusion, where some woman is making him feel good but he knows it will all end, it will all end in shame and deep sadness and horror.

"Ah," she says. "I'm sorry. Perhaps you don't like comments about your personal appearance."

"No, it's—"

"My mistake. I didn't mean to upset you. I just came because I realized I'd forgotten to ever give you a single baking lesson."

"A single baking lesson. . . ."

"I understand you're doing nicely on your own. But if you'd like a lesson or two, I can teach you."

He tries to calm down. He does, indeed, want to go to the commercial kitchen today. He can, in fact, think of nothing he'd rather do at this moment than perfect his recipe.

His face is still bright red.

He closes his eyes, sitting on the floor of the magic bathroom, and counts to 3000.

∾

The harlequin doesn't know how such an enormous change has befallen him, but it has. He's still thinking about Hylas every night, but now he also has to think about how to get money and food for himself and Falhófnir.

After the fiasco at the coffee bar, the black gelding gave him a sly look and led him to the Tasty Bread outlet behind the bus station, where they give out free bread that is past its expiration date. The harlequin takes his loaf to the stand of trees at the back of Tasty's dumpsters and crams pieces violently into his mouth. They taste terrible. He offers the rest to Falhófnir who looks Whatever but eats them all.

A homeless woman creeps up to them after they've finished the bread. She's wearing some kind of oversized musty raincoat and Bobby feels his usual disgust. He has an impulse to take off running. What does she want from him? But the woman—wow, do they really make homeless women that are 8 feet tall?—motions to Bobby and his horse, and points them to something hidden outside the bus station, something wrapped in a giant garbage bag. It is a bale of hay that has apparently fallen out of a baggage compartment and been forgotten.

∼

In the jail, no one has come to check on the prisoners in over a day. Khachiya wonders when she will be fed. She doesn't really keep track of the time in here, but it must have been quite a few mornings without food. Glenn is lonely. He wishes he were back at Salon.com and everyone adored him like the olden days. Sloppy is quivering with relief because the torture has stopped. Nehemiah is angry, as usual. "They think they can fucking just leave us alone? Fuck them!" Leslie, of course, is dead.

This morning, CO Gray rushed the door of the jailer's cell which had no lock on it and attacked his iron cot with a crowbar. "Bad jailer! Bad jailer!"

None of the corrections officers know what to do with themselves. CO Rathbaum sadly brews tea in his pot which he has recovered from beneath the jailer's cot and which thankfully Lieutenant Gray did not break when he swung the crowbar.

The others press the button on the coffee maker repeatedly, making snide remarks about the jailer all the while. They would like to play ball games with his head as the ball and watch his skull slowly shatter on the wall.

As Khachiya waits, peering at her cell door, she tries to warm herself by clutching cobwebs, for there is no blanket. THERE IS NO FOOD there is no food. Maybe it is time to eat a large, dead fly.

The slop tray in the bottom of the door opens and something slides inside. Is she hallucinating? She sees a beautiful bowl made of blue and green pottery depicting trees by a river, and inside it is a consommé that shines golden as if with the sun that she has never seen inside this place.

~

Inside Magna's house, a young person covered in blankets shivers by the fire, trying to get dry. Magna brings the young woman tea and tries to dry her sopping short hair with a towel.

"I don't go to other women to be comforted," the young woman says, frowning. "I go to other women to be excited."

The Magna who is warming the young woman in front of the fire laughs.

"It is sometimes possible to have both . . . even with the same partner," the goddess says with a twinkle in her eye.

The young woman has never felt more bratty and insolent. "Maybe if you're a hundred years old, and fuckin' ugly, like you!"

She needs to be bratty and insolent, she knows this in her innards. Because she is in peril at every moment she remains here.

CHAPTER 5

Contrarily...
In the commercial kitchen, Anna sees the jailer arrive with a very tall woman in red. Just looking at this personage makes Anna feel warm. The woman's lips are huge and scarlet, and her lipstick is bravely and boldly applied. It smells perfumed. The woman strides toward Anna, large hand outstretched. The texture and arc of the giantess's bosom makes Anna happy. Should she become a learned doctor of philosophy, to comprehend how these impossible warm parabolas of flesh hang in the air and do not fall?

Somehow she can even smell the woman's genitals, just subtly, and they too smell sweet, like evening flowers in the summer. They smell like midnight in a garden. Anna flushes a little and walks forward to take her hand.

The jailer pumps Anna on the shoulder, and looks at Magna: "This is my friend, ma'am, the one who's been helping me all this time!"

"I am very delighted to hear that!" the divine mother says, plunging her sparkling eyes into the girl's black-brown ones.

∾

Hylas has been putting off this moment as long as possible, but Jesus, it's time to leave. He has his black messenger bag, a sleek black backpack, and a string shopping bag full of fruit, bread, and cheeses ready on the landing. He's going to meet up with the rest of his mates and catch the big boat back to Upper Caspia.

He waits for a knock at the door. Sigh. Finally, he loads the bags across his shoulders, laces up his combat boots, and begins the long walk to the harbor.

He has to step through some of the least nice sections of Donnaville to get there. Men and women lie in the street, sprawled out, flies around their eyes, and teenage runaways in their underwear sidle up against him. Two large men approach him from either direction as he rounds a corner, and he has to dash between them to get away. He starts loping through the streets at a pace just under a full run, glancing behind him,scared.

~

Bobby and Falhófnir have found a place to store their hay, and an old dog blanket Bobby finally grabbed from the dump to stay warm and comfortable at night. The place is a spot in the back of an abandoned row of storage units that many of the unhoused of Donnaville have long since reclaimed. Falhófnir makes an arrangement with the keeper of the units, Mala, that she can ride him once a week in exchange for guarding their stuff.

Mala has short blond dreadlocks sticking out of a red bandanna, and a tough face that shows some acne scars. She points them to a communal pump they can get water from, then fills a huge barrelful for them herself because she's apparently really strong.

Bobby is in the middle of carefully placing garbage bags

and bits of trash around their stash to hide it, when he suddenly falls forward with a little cry.

"Aaah!"

At the same moment, Hylas, two blocks over, is hit over the head by a vampire and CO Smith. The former uses a cinderblock and the latter, his club. They take Hylas into an apartment nearby.

∼

In the kitchen, Anna has gone to check on a delivery, so Magna prances over to the jailer's stall to show him how to measure accurately. He can't quite understand it, and is growing overwhelmed and edgy. "How am I supposed to tell if it's up to the line or not? The currants don't line up precisely."

She looks at him with truly shit-eating kindness. "Eventually, you will be able to tell using just your heart."

He wants to hit her with the cast iron pan. But he doesn't know what might happen—maybe he would just wake up in the jail again?

What does he *feel* right now? he asks himself. Annoyed, frustrated, giggly, murderous?

Could he possibly be feeling fucking *yearning*? Does he want to use his actual frigging *heart*?

The jailer makes a noise somewhere between misery and a puzzled snort.

"Don't worry. You can also level it off with a spoon."

"But how am I supposed to level it off when I'm measuring liquid, say? Won't it spill over?" The jailer is in torment. Of course, he is always in torment, but today he feels it more than ever. Because he can play at being a baker all he wants, but he's about to spend another night in Donnaville away from his post. That means punishment, sure as shit. He has never once stepped off the dunghill, not in 50 years, and he's not going to now, no matter what some nice lady comes and says to him, talking sweet and patting his arm. The divine mother rubs his sweaty, hairy arm and goes off to get them some snacks.

∼

Falhófnir is concerned, because the harlequin just fell over in the street for no reason, and his head looked bloody even before he hit the ground, which didn't make sense. The horse strides up to Mala's unit and stamps his feet. When Mala comes out, muscular, short, and tattooed all over, Falhófnir whinnies pointedly.

Mala gets her med kit and listens to Bobby with her stethoscope for a moment. She laughs.

The horse is annoyed. "Don't worry, Blackie," Mala sniggers. "For some reason this dude didn't have a heart before, but a little newborn heart has just decided to take up residence in his chest. It don't look to be doing him any harm, though." She puts a cool compress on the harlequin's head and wipes the blood.

He awakens. "What?"

"You're fine, cutie pie. You don't even need a Band-Aid. Here look, no more boo-boo!" And she hands him a mirror.

∼

The harlequin likes Mala, because it's clear she isn't interested in men. He always prefers a woman who won't cling.

He can't recall that he has ever had a woman friend, because really their constant adulation gets to be too much. When women are sexual it repulses him, when they wag their breasts in his direction, especially when the nipple tips of their breasts point up and dance around, and when they're badly trying to attract him it makes him want to vomit.

Thankfully, Mala could care less. She rolls her eyes as Bobby preens in the hand mirror, making sure his hairdo still looks good combed over the red spot that bled.

∼

The prisoners are starving. Khachiya is the only one for whom soup has magically appeared, putting color in her cheeks and restoring the brightness to her dimmed brown eyes.

At home in the lush green neighborhood, Donna eats tuna salad for lunch, but follows it with peanut butter, walnuts, cherries, almonds, because she can never quite get full.

∼

The child is still on the floor in her cell that is the most hidden in Donnaville, the most intimate cell in the prison that is itself at the very heart of Donnaville. She looks uncertainly at the spot in that unshakable wall through which the jailer, every few days or so, magically appears.

"I will be good," she says very quietly. "Please let me out."

He has not come in days and she is starving. She begins

singing to herself in a sort of children's clap-game voice, keeping time softly on the iron walls.

"It stinks in there," Lieutenant Gray says, sniffing down the corridor. "Gonna flush it all out in a day or two."

∾

Back in the kitchen, the jailer is playing with chestnut cream and 26 different colors of icing. Anna and the divine mother are hanging at the little espresso/ice cream bar that the cooks have arranged for their own pleasure at a tall unoccupied central station.

An hour earlier, Magna and the jailer made their first batch of the chestnut cream. He just tasted three different versions of it that he made himself, variously honeyed, rummy, and caramelized and salty. Now he's adding a good dab of chocolate to each. On top of the bittersweet, still-warm chocolate, he paints squiggles of red, mauve, indigo, linen white, and orange icing.

Magna told him to play when she went off to chat up Anna, so yippee! he's playing. In addition to the desserts, he gets hold of some actual toys. Old brightly painted wooden ones he found in a chest in the storeroom, one that's the kind where you stack all different colored rings one on top of another, as well as slightly more complicated ones like a horsehead on a stick for him to prance around on. He's pretending now that he's a witch on a flying broomstick and he dances around his station, a flying witch, and now he sticks out his arms and zooms down the aisles all the way to the washroom.

∾

Anna is drinking a large glass of espresso with a delicious dollop of vanilla ice cream. Next to her, Magna drinks dark caramel-coffee soda with pumpkin ice cream and a few coffee beans floating in it.

"Look, he's having so much fun!" Anna says, pointing to the jailer whizzing down the aisles on his horse-stick. "Ha, he is!" says Magna, delighted.

"Has he been your friend for a long time?"

"Yeah, I've known and loved that boy about forever," says the divine mother wistfully. "But let's talk about you!" she says very gently, hand on the young woman's arm. "I hear you're wonderful at skateboarding and making hot apple pie!"

Magna's fingers on her arm feel like the sunlight on the first day of the year you can take off your coat. How did she not know about this till now?

Magna smiles like a hearth. She doesn't seem to mind that Anna cannot answer her.

"Mother, I love you."

Their kiss is long, with tongues, like velvet and metal.

∼

This is how the divine mother got the jailer to play:

The jailer is fussing and harrumphing to himself as he measures flour in a little metal cup. How can he get it to settle and line up perfectly? What if there is a tiny ridge that sticks out or falls under?

Magna hears him sighing loudly. She reaches into the air for a sack of chestnuts that weren't there before. "Jailer, I realize I've been going about this all wrong! Have you ever tasted chestnut cream?"

He remembers Christmases long ago, and marrons glacé given him by . . . someone who was definitely not his mother. "Sort of," he says. "Something like."

"The best way to make something is to love it," says the divine mother, "so I'm going to make up a batch right now and let you taste."

∾

Mala is sweeping out the sidewalk in front of the storage units when Bobby rushes up to her looking agitated. "I'm trying to find a young man," Bobby says. "He never made it to the last call for his boat."

"Do you know which way he was walking?"

"He was walking from the tourist district, towards the harbor."

"Ooh, bad one," she says. "Tourists always get rolled."

"He checked out of his guesthouse this morning," Bobby says. "Are you trying to tell me in this fucked-up little town of ours no tourist ever gets away safe?"

"I'm not trying to tell you anything, guy. Just that some streets are dangerous and nobody should go down them."

∾

The harlequin has never concerned himself with the safety of tourists before.

Of course, he has helped the city's natives flee the jail, using only their minds. He helps them fly over the prison walls, leaving just their bodies in the cells, and then he takes them on adventures, walking through marvelously fluffy fields of magenta flowers, enormous zinnias and marigolds on stalks as tall as people, and the people fleeing the jail clutch the creamy huge petals to their face and they inhale the scent of the flowers like rank sweaty honey and they leave their bodies behind, usually, like poor Raya, for the jailer to toss on the trash heap.

∼

The child in the innermost room is listening to her own music as she sings and taps on the walls with her hands and feet.

"Oh little playmate
Come out and play with me
And bring your dollies three
Climb up my apple tree
Slide down my rain barrel
Into my cellar door
And we'll be jolly friends
Forevermore, 1234!"

The harlequin hears her, and materializes in her cell playing the clap-game with her. For a second she's delighted—she can't believe she gets to clap against the harlequin's much larger hands and feet—then she shakes her head slowly.

"No, I don't want to do that," says the child. "I want to get out of here in real life, with my body and everything."

The harlequin frowns. The children and adults that he helps free don't usually understand the game as well as this one does.

"That's much harder," he says.

"Maybe we just need some help," says the girl. "Whom shall we call on?"

∽

The jailer has stretched his two arms out like eagles' wings, and he is quietly, happily "flying" around the back of the commercial kitchen. He wishes he had feathers.

Some of the cooks think he's strange, but then again, cooks as a whole are a pretty strange group of people. In fact, they recognize this about themselves, which sometimes makes them more tolerant of odd birds like the jailer.

Anna comes up and taps him on a wing. "Hi!"

"Hi!" The jailer is super-animated, more animated than anyone has seen him except maybe Leslie and Glenn. "I'm enjoying flying!"

"I can see that."

"DO YOU LIKE FLYING TOO?" Now he is rounding with his wings faster, faster and faster, whispering hi to his friend the Sun and waving at all the mountains he has never seen before out the window.

"YEAH!" Anna shouts. "I LOVE IT!"

Then "HEY!" she says. "I'VE BEEN MEANING TO ASK YOU A QUESTION!"

The jailer drops speed gradually, wings still out, coming to rest finally at his friend's clavicle. He says softly: "Hello there, Anna!"

"What is your name?"

The jailer winks. "Come outside with me a moment, will you?"

∽

They stand in the stinky alley where the cooks go to smoke, and Anna brings out a stick of violet gum for each of them.

"I don't know my own name," he says, "but most people call me the jailer."

Anna tastes her own bile.

"You're the jailer? Do you mean to say that you're the guy in charge of the prison?"

"Well, I retired a day and a half ago."

Anna's face has an expression on it that he's never seen on anybody's face before.

"You tortured people. What the fuck is wrong with you?"

∼

E comes out to where Donna is sitting in the backyard, bringing her a lunch she made: braised short-rib chili, still warm, with bread to dunk in it. Donna looks up: E has also baked her some prediabetic-friendly cookies, wrapped in a little bag. E's lips are painted scarlet, and as she kisses Donna over the table, Donna feels her breasts brush her, takes in her warm, spicy perfume. Being kissed by E is like being kissed by a goddess of the ocean and the wavy dunes and a wetland garden heating up with water lilies and honeysuckle and lotus. It makes Donna feel like Bottom, in *A Midsummer Nights Dream*, being kissed by Titania, the queen of the fairies. Bottom, while he's being kissed, has a giant donkey's head on instead of his own. Ee-aww, he goes, Ee-aww, as the majestic fairy queen caresses his cheek and strokes his furry skin and kisses him.

∼

Back at the storage-room encampment, the harlequin and Mala are sharing a single hard-boiled egg, trying to figure out what to do.

He left the little girl in jail for one quick second and flew off to consult Mala in the blink of an eye.

But despite Mala's obvious competence, he's not feeling very secure about the little girl's situation, in that scorching hamster cage with no food. "We have to act fast, and I mean fast," he tells Mala.

She chews on her half of the egg thoughtfully. "Gotta call Magna, babes. Either that or find the jailer himself."

∼

The jailer motions Anna to sit on some littered vegetable crates while he tries to calculate various possible scenarios for making her like him again.

"I've always been a public servant," he begins. "I really care about the—"

Anna gets up and walks down the dirty alley, reaches the street and begins walking rapidly away.

∼

"Who the fuck is Magna?" the harlequin asks.

Mutual incomprehension.

"You're 56 years old and you don't know who she is yet?"

"How did you know my age?" He's very angry.

Mala grins unpleasantly. "I'm a smart woman."

No one has guessed his real age in decades. Finally he says grudgingly: "Can you tell me anything about her?"

"You must've met her at some point. Actually I thought you'd really like her, being as into sex and beauty as you are."

"Now you fucking know everything about me?" The harlequin is so mad he is conjuring an actual storm, he is on his feet and generating a storm made of anger that is suddenly smashing rain and hailstones down onto Mala's encampment from the sky. He hears her murmur, from the shelter of a storage container: "That child will be gone tomorrow."

∼

The divine mother is back home. Honey runs through her body as she remembers Anna's hand squeezing her shoulders. But all at once she recalls that little girl in the inmost cell, and reaches with her mind into that terrible place she was singing to, and tries to grasp . . . tries to grasp the child's hand. But can't. Around the cell's psychic habitation, gates of adamantine iron will not let her in.

So much in Donnaville still will not open to her, does not like her, hates her voice. (No matter whether conscious, adult Donna takes the wax out of her ears or not.) The harlequin is not the only denizen of Donnaville who finds Magna disgusting, excessive, dirty.

Finds her hateful, murderous, horrible!

Magna thinks about how to get inside those gates, how to slither under them or seep inside like gas.

∼

Bobby asks, "How do I find this Magna?"

Mala smirks. "She's all around you, babes."

Just then, Falhófnir canters in from a very special moment with a female friend from his old stable (because geldings, *contra* the hopes of torturers everywhere, can and do have sex). Falhófnir's ears are pitched forward, and he seems interested in Bobby and Mala's conversation. He keeps nudging the back of Bobby's head with his nose.

Bobby ignores Falhófnir. He tells the little butch woman, "I don't know about chasing after Magna. What if we just track down the jailer instead?"

∼

That individual, however, wants to die.

The jailer has often wanted to die before, but he's never been a person who's allowed to just lay down his responsibilities that way.

It's all gone. Everything I hoped for. Anna knows who I am, and what I do.

I haven't ever had a friend like that before, someone who would agree to see me just because they liked me. Just because they wanted to have a drink or a bit of warmth with me and talk about life.

I spoiled it because I was too greedy, thought too much of myself. It was the one time I thought someone might actually like to stick their hands right into that sodden rubbish pile at the center of me. But why would anybody want to do that?

∼

"Don't you have to find your friend as well?" Mala's asking the harlequin.

"Oh shit." Bobby knew his brain was not well organized, but could he actually have forgotten about his poor, missing Hylas?

Yes. Yes indeedy. Could have forgotten about him, and did. His mother always told him he was selfish.

"Time really matters in these situations."

"Let's go find these people—" the harlequin starts decisively.

Mala interrupts, "Jailer's better if we have to feel around inside the criminal underworld."

~

Anna is disturbed. Her roommate asks, "You're crying about Your Father's Oldsmobile?"

That was what they'd called the jailer whenever they talked about him, because Anna had described him as "that really nice old guy who smelled like shit one day."

"Your Father's Oldsmobile turns out to be the head of the fucking prison."

"Ooh!" Frank's acne'd face lights up, because for once he has good gossip. "They say he just walked out of the Inner Jail two days ago and never came back! He left them all in the lurch and nobody knows why. The guards are freaked, and I mean FREAKED."

Anna's tight, pink face goes through a complicated maneuver. Frank looks arch. "They might have to let everybody out."

~

Hylas wakes and finds that he can't move his arms or legs. He seems to be shackled to a bed.

There is butternut squash purée on his stomach, and the rest of him is naked.

When he hears someone entering the room, he closes his eyes and pretends to be asleep. The person moves thin, strong hands slowly and gradually over his face, with a horrible persistence, examining, examining . . . what?

"Cheekbones are better." Then, louder, to an unseen person: "You know that it's YOUR dangly nuts on the chopping block if he stays plain!"

"I'm not plain," Hylas whispers to himself.

∽

Falhófnir bumps his rump into the harlequin's chest.

"WHAT?"

He bumps his rump into Bobby's chest again. The harlequin looks at the horse, annoyed.

"So you want me to contact . . . *this divine mother person??*"

Neigh-eigh-eigh . . . !!

"Where exactly would we find, *this, ah, Mommy??*"

∽

The jailer, still in his new leather duds but no longer looking cute or cool, bumps down the street, moving slowly. This eagle ain't flying no more.

"Mr. Jailer!" says a musical voice. It is V. Maedda the grocer, out to dance or to do calisthenics by the looks of their outfit. "How did the tea work out?" they say.

"It was pretty good," the jailer says gruffly.

"Don't you think you should drink some more?"

"I'm done brewing tea, you ugly little fag-dyke."

V. Maedda gives the jailer a long look. It is simultaneously detached, compassionate, and firm. The jailer has had almost no experience with a look like that. V. Maedda, gazing at him directly, says, "You will never call anyone that again."

"Who's going to make me?"

"We all will."

"You can't make me do fucking shit!"

And V. Maedda raises their arms and the jailer is suddenly enveloped in a cool peppermint mist in a kind of funnel shape that lifts him off the ground and he feels himself, higher and higher, zooming dangerously up through the clouds on a peppermint tornado.

∾

Falhófnir impatiently motions with his muzzle for Bobby to get on his back. He takes off like a shot towards the river, but once they get to its little beach the gelding's forward lope veers even more forward and higher, becomes suddenly diagonal, and . . . *"Where the fuck are you taking me?"* screams the harlequin. For they are definitely flying, up and up over the river toward the clouds, up now over the hills on the western bank, they fly higher and higher and now the harlequin is screaming *"I'm burning! I am going to melt!"* The gelding grimaces at him, and just as it looks like they are about to fly into the Sun, he bears slightly low and to the right and they land on a queer sort of mountain fortress. Bobby can't tell if it's made of glass or grass or starlight. Falhófnir dives down inside the glimmering place, and they are in a country with big silver-barked trees and animals hopping and flying all around.

In a clearing with a large emerald-green house, there is a bonfire going in the backyard. Falhófnir elegantly sets down at the side of the fire and the harlequin just as elegantly steps off, having recovered some of his élan.

A tall woman walking with a slow dignity comes out to meet them. In one hand, she is holding a flaming candelabra, and in the other, a mess of pumpkin seeds. "Welcome, my guests. It's rare that anyone has come to meet me in my own country."

"We need you!" says the harlequin, who then clamps his teeth shut, shocked to hear this bizarro horseshit coming from his own mouth.

∼

The young woman, the one who Magna had been comforting and drying by the fire, has been sleeping in all day and wakes now, horrified by her need to see the goddess again. There is a raging in her crotch, and her breasts need to be touched.

The room she is in is irritatingly bland, with little doilies underneath the nightstand lamp and some weird bric-a-brac on the bureau, something that could either be a replica of an old sailing ship or an abstract wooden model of the clitoris. She gets up, opens the French doors, and squirming and aching from her head to her tailbone, goes out to the bonfire.

"Well now!" says Magna. "I'm really happy you could join us around the fire. Sweetie, this is Bobby."

"That's not my friggin' name!" The young man sitting on a lovely leather settee near the goddess is indignant.

"Ah now, sure," says the goddess. "So what's your name, then, love?"

CHAPTER 6

When the terrifying, skinny person talking to Dangly Nuts leaves the room, Hylas calms his mind and tries to move the parts of his body he is able to. He tightens and relaxes his stomach muscles, his face muscles, and his butt, shimmies his hips as much as he can. In Upper Caspia, they do a form of qi gong known as the Golden Leaf—a nice old lady three houseboats over taught it to him last year. He does the slow, deliberate neck rolls that the woman taught him, then tries to wiggle his toes as much as the chain will allow.

He misses the harlequin with a kind of fretful regret, but most of all he misses his neighbors and friends in Upper Caspia, the old lady, the people who bake him sourdough and care for him.

∼

In the prison, Glenn is cold. He's been left naked, and he tries to rub himself against his cot and the bare walls. He mourns his late husband in Rio, misses his children and dogs. He didn't ask to live in Donnaville rent-free, and he starts to knock his feet against the walls to make some noise, trying to do so in a way that won't hurt him. The walls are made of lead that has been made thrice as hard as normal. Then he begins humming and singing to add to the sound.

From a place Glenn can't see, Khachiya sings back, and

stamps her own feet against her cell walls. Nehemiah responds, clanging. He must have secreted a cardboard paper towel roll or something, because he's keeping time now, banging it against the metal, yelling loudly, like a kind of angry jazz.

∽

"I'm not telling you my fucking name," the harlequin says.

"That is no problem," Magna says. "But how should we address you when we talk to you?"

"I shouldn't have come." Now the harlequin is standing to his full height. On his face is the look of contempt he reserves for every individual with a body shaped like Magna's. He has finally realized where he saw her before. Why is that musty homeless lady from the bus station some kind of big shot here? How can she be the goddess he was seeking?

He can definitely smell vagina now, seeping out from the bottom of her ancient Greek-style dress. The smell is cloying, a little sweeter than he expected but still the most obvious vagina stink he's ever encountered. And he's supposed to bow and scrape in front of that?

She, for the first time in his brief acquaintance, looks a little sad and lost.

∽

"I need you!" the young woman says angrily, moving her hips.

Back in the meadow, Falhófnir rears.

"I need you too, my love," Magna replies sadly, stroking the girl's hair. The latter frowns, but begins stroking the goddess's lower thighs aggressively in response, too zealously, even punishingly, moving upward. Magna's face is abruptly red and happy, if a little too intense. Bobby says to no one in particular, "What are they doing?"

∼

It is early the next morning, and milky sunlight fills the commercial kitchen. The jailer's station is empty, but his batches of chestnut cream fill the refrigerator. Anna is thinking she effectively banished him because she simply couldn't imagine that the notorious warden of Donnaville's prison and her shy, gentle friend were actually one and the same person.

Yet they were one and the same.

What had she refused to hear when he had spoken?

What had she been unwilling to comprehend?

Should she have reported him to the army of the poor that was even now, Frank said, scouring the city for him?

∼

The child sighs in her iron cell, because it is morning. The harlequin still hasn't returned. Nor has Daddy, the man who strikes and feeds her. She misses him. What if she never sees him again, those dark eyes and that eager face? It may be hard to believe, but he is the only human regularly in her life, and sometimes she misses him more than eating.

∼

Up in his peppermint tornado, the jailer looks down on the city numbly as the twister lifts him skyward. Hard by the slums, he notes the pee-soaked public plaza where the brother and sister exchange sex for food. It's a process that has always, frankly, interested him. Then he's flying directly over the art museums, the tourist district, and the beautiful neighborhood by the river. Finally he can feel the prison, as the tornado roars above it, can feel his charge, the child, inside it whimpering as usual. She is hungry, and he is supposed to hit her and feed her. It has been like this every day for 50 years. Now he is flying at 110 miles an hour into a dark enormous cloud and he feels guilt burn him like an acid. He's supposed to be that angry cloud for the child, that dark, swirling necessary presence. How will she survive his absence?

∼

In the beautiful emerald fortress, Falhófnir is eating the most delicious mush of his life, a kind of oats grown in heaven, mixed with starlight and maple syrup.

The young woman—let's call her Kleine—continues to stroke the goddess, who has become half-recumbent on her outdoor chaise lounge and is trying to keep her head up and herself polite to all three of her guests at once as she receives this tender worship.

The harlequin is feeling the oddest, most uncomfortable sensation. All at once he *wants* the goddess, wants her from the pit of his being, the depths of his lungs, bowels, base of his prostate. And he is jealous, jealous of Kleine for getting to stroke her *there*, in that place of fire, the center of the Lady's heat and power and feeling.

∼

The brother can't speak louder than a whisper anymore because he has been punched in the throat one too many times. But in his sure, thin growl he says, "It's time to rush the prison."

His sister answers in her usual wry tone, "Almost." Spring is officially here now.

They are middle-aged but strangely youthful, maybe because they're both are so skinny. Their many followers have brought the legendary pair new-to-them black clothes, not that dirty or torn, and V. Maedda brings beans, cheese, and corn once a week. Every sunset, people discreetly gather near them, but the prison guards have begun to notice and last night a few went among them savagely with some metal batons. An officer had edged much too close to the sister then, put a hand on her waist, and whispered, "Tomorrow night we'll bring a vampire in. How do you think you'll like that?"

∽

Up in the tornado, the jailer panics. He is going higher, higher, and his limbs are splayed. His body starts to turn over and over in a circle and he gapes at the furious darkness all around him, afraid of what might be spinning around on top of him that could break him into bits. Then the tornado slows abruptly, and he's terrified. But the twister, decelerating, gently unfurls him in a column of air and, slackening queerly more and more, deposits him almost tenderly down on velvety grass. When he gets to his feet, the tornado is gone.

"Mr. Jailer!" the goddess hails him excitedly from her fuchsia lounger.

∼

Anna is baking handheld apple pies. It is her life's work, and her attention will never not be caught by the task of making apples taste crazy wonderful in an elegant tiny pastry dress. She has experimented with lemon juice and even blood orange and red grapefruit with the apple filling, with the very hottest and spiciest kind of cinnamon, with cumin even, with sweet cream and sour. She has had her fun with pecans, hazelnuts, cashews, and peanuts. Lately, she's been playing with different kinds of dough. A restaurant has just asked her to make phyllo apple pies with sour cream and walnuts, which has her absolutely thrilled as, at this very moment, she is rolling out—on her own rented steel counter!—the first homemade phyllo dough of her life.

She doesn't even think of the jailer again until her break.

∼

"Magna," the jailer says dully. "What are you doing here?"

"It's you who have come to MY country, sweet love. But I've always wanted you to visit me."

Kleine hasn't stopped finger-fucking the goddess as the latter greets the jailer from her chaise lounge.

Bobby, on the other side of her, keeps watching the fucking and occasionally lurches in to stroke the goddess's neck or affectionately to rub her feet.

Falhófnir is getting hot under the collar again, in between bouts of his own laughter. He paws the ground sweatily, harrumphing.

"Magna," says the jailer, "what is going on?"

Magna tries to concentrate in between moans. She detaches herself from the other two humans temporarily and sits up. "The child needs you, jailer. She is at great risk today, right now, this minute." Then she turns to the harlequin: "My darling boy, she needs you, too."

∼

It is a pale morning at the prison, filtering in through the dirty windows. Lieutenant Gray, sporting a considerably hipper haircut, meets with his officers: Smith, Rathbaum, Auxiliary Pepowitz, and Anxious, plus a couple of vampires recruited from the downtown cosmetics project.

"Today we wash out that little thing in the iron room, then we go for the rabble in the plaza."

∼

The jailer forces himself to concentrate, because something inside him is making him very sleepy. Something else is making him feel GOOD in a way he hasn't in years and he knows it's wrong, but he wants so badly just to reach out and touch inside the goddess's vagina, which smells like that hot, spicy cinnamon.

"Let me get you some coffee," the goddess is saying, and she flits into her house. Bobby and Kleine follow and come out again immediately with a hot pitcher of coffee. They all drink, except Falhófnir.

Then the jailer sits deliberately down in one of Magna's wicker chairs and tries to PAY ATTENTION in a way he hasn't in 50 years. He looks into the goddess's eyes, trying to keep awake. He pinches the sensitive flesh between his thumb and forefinger. "What exactly is going on with my child?"

"They're going to kill her today. Soon."

Bobby is dreamy, still in a reverie of the goddess's juices. "They're not supposed to kill her. They're supposed to keep her there forever, unless just her spirit escapes with me."

Magna looks agonized and annoyed at once. "Well, they're going to kill her. And no, I don't want them to keep her forever, either. And no, I don't want just her spirit to escape with you."

The jailer is almost back to sleep, and his voice is dopey. "We're not supposed to kill her. We're supposed to make her better."

The divine mother is better at controlling herself than most. She breathes in calm, clean air and just manages it. Then she fixes on the jailer's hazel eyes firmly: "But you haven't really been making her better, have you?"

"That . . . that's been my whole purpose in life. Isn't she better?"

∽

"No," says the harlequin. "Her life is shit. Brother."

"W-Who are you?"

Bobby laughs. "You haven't been able to see me for many years, have you, brother?"

What. No, fuck, it can't be. The jailer hasn't thought about the younger brother he loves, the younger brother he tried to protect, for a very long time.

"You can't be him. He died. I saw him leave his body when his head fell to the floor."

"I never died, babe." The harlequin is cracking up. "I've been thwarting you and thumbing my nose at you for 50 years. I could see you, but you were never, ever, ever able to see me."

Kleine bursts out: "Apparently someone else is about to die, so could you please put a lid on the family reunion for now?"

∼

In the end, three riders set out from the emerald fortress, Bobby on Falhófnir and the jailer and young Kleine on the goddess's two llamas.

Kleine expects the goddess to be mad she's joining in the sortie. But out of the corner of her eye, she just sees Magna looking surreptitiously proud.

The jailer is afraid he may break the llama's back because he's so heavy. Sensuality, however, trots over to him with determination and crouches down until he sets his legs on either side of her sturdy, chunky body.

Kleine winds her fingers into Delight's mane. Oh my God, he is creamy white, velvety, a marvel.

"What are you, a 10-year-old girl?" Bobby rolls his eyes at her. "Drawing pictures of unicorns and rainbows all over your notebook?"

∼

Once they're airborne, Falhófnir gives him a chilly glance.

"I know this is important!" Bobby screeches in a heavy stage whisper. "But why did these *yutzes* have to join in?"

∼

On the llama's back, in the air, the jailer is talking to himself: "I didn't betray him."

"Yes you did."

"No I didn't."

"You made him stay in the house."

"It was safer there."

"No it wasn't."

"He was bad."

"You hurt him!"

"I did that to protect him from our parents!"

"It wasn't fucking successful!"

At that point, instead of continuing this conversation, the jailer just mimes talking and hits himself in the head. Then he mimes talking again and hits himself back.

Underneath him, Sensuality finally intervenes. While continuing to fly, she starts dancing and shaking her tushy so hard—while covertly keeping good firm hold of him—that the jailer is frightened out of his internal dialogue. He's afraid of falling. They are over the residential neighborhood now, with its vast tall trees through which, still bare, you can see the mountains.

Kleine decides to talk to the harlequin. "So, are you under the goddess's care, too?"

"No, I'm not under her goddamned care!" He turns his face away, shamed. He can't believe that, after resisting the goddess for so long, he now likes, wants, needs the Empress Of The Sacred Vulva Glow. He feels as though he's been made to go down on his mother. And worse than that, likes it.

∼

In the prison, all the prisoners are banging on the walls. Nehemiah has managed to make a hole in his cell wall and is reaching his long arm out through it to waggle it at the guards. "Ha ha! Ha ha! Got my arm through that hole! I got you, I got you, assholes!"

With exploding laughter, he starts flinging his shit out through the hole so that any guard who comes by will get painted in it.

In the station room, the officers are still enjoying the top-quality donuts and coffee that Lieutenant Gray secured special for today, but the lieutenant is going to start the show soon.

Still in the air, Kleine sees that the jailer has stopped hitting himself. She dares to move in closer. "I don't believe we've met."

"I am the jailer," he screws up his wrinkly face because he doesn't think he should be allowed to hold this title any longer, "young lady."

"I'm Kleine."

"I think you are even younger than my brother over there." He motions to the harlequin, now lavishly rolling his back and shoulders on the horse and trying to pet him with the backs of his hands.

"A little younger." The three are cruising over the rooftops now, looking for a place to land.

Sensuality and Delight look at Falhófnir, and without needing to exchange any further communication, all three animals are decided: They're not landing until a particular something happens.

After trying and failing to alight on the roof of a nightclub, Bobby notices: "What's wrong? Why can't we land?"

The jailer tries to nudge Sensuality downward with his thighs, but the chunky llama isn't letting him make landfall, either. "These beasts are waiting for something," he tells the younger two.

"They're waiting for us to come up with a plan!" Kleine bursts out. "We can't just land on top of the jail without a strategy, we barely even know each other."

"We have to get the kid out," the harlequin says. The jailer nods, once. The harlequin goes on in his beautiful tenor, as though he were singing a jingle: "We should get the other prisoners out, too."

"Where do we take them afterward?" asks Kleine. "They won't all fit on our animals, how do we get them away from the site? How do we stop the guards from killing anyone? Jailer, don't you know how this place works? Shouldn't you be the one devising the plan?"

One more responsibility, the jailer growls to himself. *Even when I set my responsibilities down, they're always going to give the good ol' jailer one more responsibility to make up for it.* Aloud, he grouses: "Why am *I* always in charge?"

"Okay, I'll come up with the plan," says Kleine. "Jailer, where is the little girl being held? Can we get there without being attacked?"

"I will sing them all to sleep," says the harlequin, "if the jailer will just show us where to go."

CHAPTER 7

The harlequin casts his arms wide as soon as they land on the bleak little street in front of the prison. The jail is disguised as a grand old bank that has long since shuttered. But almost everyone in Donnaville knows exactly where it is. There is no guard outside, because the guards have never imagined anyone crazy enough to break in.

The harlequin starts a dancing motion, drawing figure eights with his arms and raking his legs long from side to side. It looks like a cross between an Irish jig and an invigorating Polish folk dance. Then he begins to clap and sing, and the other two are startled by his soaring voice and lack of embarrassment.

He goes up the outer steps. Then he opens the door to the abandoned bank, still crooning and sweeping his legs, and continues singing as he jigs inside. Kleine and the jailer follow him in.

Falhófnir, Sensuality, and Delight stay outside on the street, backs to the door like sentinels.

The jail lies backward a good ways, through the entire lobby of the old bank. Under the soaring arches of the main teller's hall, the jailer and Kleine trail behind a little. They find that they are also skipping and dancing, as the harlequin continues jigging all the way to the back.

"I don't know what my legs are doing," says the jailer, looking wonderingly down at his extensions. He hasn't danced, even a little, since he was five. As the jailer twirls on the floor, he can see that the great hall is dusty. He has very seldom cleaned in the anteroom to the prison. Makes a note to punish himself for it later that night.

At the very back, Bobby opens the door to the stairs that go down to the bank vault, but instead of going down that way he does a neat sideways movement, through a door almost no one can see. Kleine and the jailer follow him through, and then they are at the guards' station.

In that instant, Lieutenant Gray, Smith, Rathbaum, Pepowitz, and Anxious all look up, chewing donuts, but the harlequin half sings half chants, "Oh my darling, I want to put lipstick on you, beautiful red lipstick on all your faces, I want to perfume you, jasmine and musk at your ears," and within half a moment they are all in trance, eyes staring open as their minds flip shut.

"Quick, Jailer!" calls Kleine. "Where is the child?"

The jailer, a look on his face of combined unease, regret, and shame with many, even contradictory causes, points vaguely to the back of the station room. That room is a messy office full of files, broken-down desk chairs, and old coffee stains, and they see the jailer gesturing halfheartedly at one of its piss-colored walls. But then he strides in the direction of a tiny grease spot on the wall, and the other two follow. The jailer walks straight through the spot on the wall, then Kleine walks through, then the harlequin steps through the piss-paint on the outside but is almost caught, is almost trapped inside the pulsating, cold-hot, red-white-black vibrating wall until at last he squeezes through.

"What was that?" he asks the jailer accusingly.

"It's meant to keep the Lady out," the jailer mutters, abashed. "You are like her, so it almost kept you out, too."

"I am like her??"

"Guys!" says Kleine, and runs over to the middle of the rather large cell, where the child, eyes closed, is walking around with her arms outstretched and her legs spread out at large angles, imitating a starfish. She is 3 1/2 feet tall with dirty-blond to brown hair, and naked. Her movement is beautiful and dancelike, and they pause to watch her.

But "Jerkwad!" the jailer cries, "What the fuck are you doing?" and he runs in and hits her in the head with both fists.

Kleine moves faster than she would've thought possible. She grabs the jailer's arms and pins them as Bobby gently sweeps up the child and pulls her to his chest. "Hey, you're back," the girl turns in Bobby's arms to look him in the face, delighted. "You returned in real life!"

Then she calls over to the jailer in the corner with Kleine, "Don't worry, Daddy, I was waiting for you too!"

"Dumbass!" he says. "You're not ever entitled to wait for me. I know you've been fucking up while I was gone." And he meanders out of Kleine's grip and walks over slowly, menacingly to the warmer half of the room where Bobby is hugging the little girl.

Kleine and the harlequin lock eyes. In a split second, she has clamped the jailer's arms behind his back again, and Bobby breathes once slowly, deliberately, almost luxuriously into the jailer's face. The older man falls asleep, lets his head and even his body fall to the filthy floor, and sucks his thumb.

"What happened to Daddy?" the little girl asks.

"He just got very tired and needed a nap," the harlequin tells her, stroking her hair.

∼

They have a problem.

Bobby signs the words to Kleine, so that the child will not understand. How will all four of them get back through the wall?

Who will go first, and what if the harlequin gets stuck? Which one of them will make sure the jailer and the child get through, too?

"The jailer's still asleep, so we should push him through first. He should be okay out there," Kleine signs rapidly.

The child notices the signing and imitates them. "Are we dancing with our arms now?"

"You go after the jailer," Kleine signs, "and I will walk through holding the girl."

∼

Hylas, the harlequin's love interest, wakes up and finds himself free of restraints, on a creamy white couch. The room is luxurious, with bright sunlight flooding in and a liquor cabinet off to the side. A handsome man with long hair, almost an animal in the thick pelted hair all over his body, strides over to him naked and rubs the top of his head.

"Do you have everything you need?"

"I—I would like some water and food."

The elegant hairy man disappears into an alcove and returns with fresh-baked bread and butter and a jug of sparkling water with limes and some cups.

"I don't understand," Hylas makes himself say aloud. The door, he notices, is thick and covered in leather, a more beautiful door than anywhere Bobby ever took him.

"It's all going to be okay, Bonbon." The hairy man pours water for them both.

Hylas looks down and realizes that for the first time in many days, he's wearing clothes. They are not his own clothes, however. He is wearing a chic Parisian dress with a large print of blue lines and triangles, the most expensive and fashionable thing he has ever had on.

∼

The brother and sister crawl on their bellies for six blocks, all the way to the former bank. Have they just taken their begging to a whole new level of theatricality, or is this some kind of protest? Their clothes are torn, sure, and like always, they are hungry. But this famous pair have never been known to abase themselves, even when asking for money. "Is it performance art?" someone asks. From a block away, a few office workers and businessmen and -women are looking at the activists and pointing.

In the jail, Sloppy is sick of waiting for food. He was the jailer's second favorite, next to the child. Which meant he got fed more than the others but he also got hurt more.

There is a permanent, round, livid hole in the joints of his right leg and his left shoulder from the jailer trying to get him to walk better, make a system of him. Now he sees where his own jail cell, not made of lead like the others but mostly wood, has been similarly weakened. Abruptly, he smashes his strong right arm through a visible hole in the wall. The structure of the cell has been so decayed from the jailer's frequent visits that it collapses, wood flying everywhere. As it turns out, the jailer was so eager to correct Sloppy he just stuck plywood onto the walls whenever they failed so he could visit frequently, without breaks for reconstruction.

∼

When the harlequin walks back through the child's cell wall, he feels hands grabbing at him, mouths sucking and nipping to keep him in that in-between place. The mouths are enormous and red, and he can smell the hamster-smell now, how could he have possibly not smelled it before, coming from the cage of that little girl who has not been washed in years?

But behind him, Kleine has entered the wall and she is pushing him, pushing him with what turn out to be surprisingly strong arms past all the mouths. The little girl is hanging on her chest.

Then they are out, the jailer still dead asleep, on the dusty floor of the station room. Kleine, the harlequin, and the child find themselves moving through a scene of frozen guards. For Gray, Smith, Rathbaum, Pepowitz, and Anxious remain motionless—some seated, some hovering over the donut box. Bobby props the jailer up against a wall because he and his two compatriots need a moment.

"What's your name, honey?"

"I'm just 'The Child,' " the child says helpfully.

Bobby smiles at her. "That's a great name."

Kleine says, "Hey, I brought some pumpkin seeds for you," and she digs them out of her jeans jacket, a napkin full of them that Kleine saved from the little party at Magna's bonfire. The child's eyes widen, and she stuffs them fast into her mouth.

Bobby, after a thoughtful second, takes his shirt off and puts it on the child. It's purple silk, and on her big enough for a dress.

∽

Sloppy is out, now that his cell has crumpled into nothing. The others can hear him singing and moving around freely in the hall. Nehemiah's hand, still covered in the shit he has been flinging, does a high-five in the air as he screams in celebration, SLOPPY!! MY BOY!! Glenn's voice takes on a brutally haranguing tone: "You're just going to abandon us now, aren't you? Like the neoliberal shill you are."

Sloppy's voice is gentle as he answers: "No, I am not going to abandon you." Instead, he goes around to each of the cells in turn and unlocks them. Nehemiah appears to be a pair of lips surrounded by a hulking body made entirely of shit. Khachiya somehow is still wearing makeup and a dress fashionable in 2020 Moscow. Glenn looks like a desiccated fish body extending down from a skull.

Sloppy pulls each of them out into the foyer. Nehemiah jumps up and pumps his shoulder with a shitty fist. Khachiya thanks him seriously and blows a kiss. Glenn, too weak to sit up, tries to make his facial muscles do a sneer.

"Where's Leslie?" suddenly it occurs to Sloppy to ask.

"She's been gone for days," says Glenn scathingly. "Weren't you paying attention?"

∽

As much as I, Donna, personally hate Glenn, he is a resident of Donnaville because he is part of me. So, how can he be part of me if he's a real-life journalist who lives in Brazil? You do the math.

One of the reasons I hate him is I am also (at times) a petulant, hypercritical person who cannot distinguish between my own compulsions and the needs of the world.

∾

"How are we going to push him through this entire prison and out the door?" Kleine is asking. "Do we even WANT to get the jailer out of here? Maybe this is where he belongs."

The child is watching Kleine and the harlequin sharply as they sign.

"I just have the sense that it's better if he leaves the prison," Bobby says, combing the child's hair. "He's not supposed to be here. None of them are."

"Okay, well, how are we going to push him out of here and also free the other inmates?"

"First things first," the harlequin says. "First we open all the other cages and free the others, then we push the jailer out into the open air!"

At that very moment, three vampires burst open the door from the bank and leap inside. Kleine and the shirtless harlequin instinctively wrap their bodies around the child, so the vampires, in black T-shirts and jeans, with huge fangs, seize the jailer instead and bite him.

∾

Bobby signals frantically to Kleine, who takes the child. Bobby takes a deep breath and, jumping terrified to where the vampires are, begins kissing them.

They let the jailer fall against a chair and surround the harlequin, greedy for his hot little mouth. The vampires have never encountered lips as red and drunken-looking as his. Bobby kisses them all in turn and the vampires also kiss each other, the vamps are getting hot as they have not for years and now their shirts are coming off, they are beautiful men but very thin. All four of them are in a pile on the floor sucking and licking, and the harlequin catches Kleine's eye as soon as he can and silently tells her *Run.*

With one arm around the child and the other propelling the jailer forward, Kleine hustles them both out of the room. But she cannot find the magic sideways door and so she ends up down another corridor, where the smell of filth is so startling and frightening, she can barely make herself walk.

As she looks ahead, cobwebs larded with insects stretch over dank, uncertain rooms, and a greasy, hazy, toxic-smelling film hangs over the air.

Kleine would have thought she wouldn't mind filth, because she loves transgression. "Women doing filthy things to her, because she is filthy." In other words, because she's human, or because she's a woman, or because she wants sex. But now she sees that when it comes right down to it, she doesn't want to be treated as though she were filthy. People do bad things to people they don't let wash.

Holding her two charges, she cautiously rounds a bend and comes face to face with four dirty people. Two are standing, one is sitting, and one with a sneer on his filthy face is lying down.

∼

All day, the divine mother has been trying to whittle out more little creatures of wood and failing. They look lumpy. They don't have the right kind of noses, the right sorts of lungs, how will they be able to breathe? Their legs are not adequate to support them. She keeps scrapping them and starting over.

She misses Bobby, Kleine, and the jailer.

"I know you're worried about them," her raven, Introspection, tells her.

"They are in a lot of danger."

"Take a break," Introspection says. "Kiss a girl. Why don't you go look up Anna and eat her pie all day?"

∼

A giant man covered in shit grabs the jailer around the neck before Kleine can react. "Is he dead, or just sleeping?"

"He's out for a while. What are you—"

The one woman, bizarrely decked out in cosmetics over the dirt, gets up from where she is sitting and kicks the jailer in the balls. On the floor, the dead-fish-looking guy lifts an elbow fast and rams the jailer in the knees.

"Stop it!" yells the child.

The fourth stranger in the corridor, who has not lifted a hand to the jailer yet, looks at the child curiously and crouches down to her level. "Why?" he asks seriously. "Why should we stop hitting him?"

"Because he's my Daddy. And, we need him."

"Well, he's kind of my Daddy too," says Sloppy, thinking. "But I'm not sure that should make us be gentle necessarily—"

"I hate you!" says Nehemiah, smearing shit from his own skin all over the jailer's body. He takes some off his massive arms, off his huge, muscular thighs, and bedecks his former torturer. The jailer wakes up, sniffing himself. "What . . . You're out of the cells—"

Nehemiah headbutts him and stomps on his knees. When the jailer topples over, hitting his head, Khachiya bites him on the face and neck. "Bastard! Shithead!"

"Stop this." Kleine has been wavering in the last few seconds about what to do. But *I have to act,* she thinks. "He's my charge," she announces in a clear, cool voice, "and I'm bringing him out of this prison. I'm here to bring the rest of you out, too, if you want." She put an arm around the old man and starts pulling him hard, with muscle power, away from the two cramped, dirt-covered people.

"Nah, we're taking him away to torture him." It's Glenn, who stands quickly. He grabs the jailer from the other side, towering over him and 5 foot two Kleine. He sinks his long teeth into the jailer's throat, puncturing it, a look of relief suddenly on his face—

A single, high, strange note abruptly rings out: "Ahhhhhhhh!" Glenn, Sloppy, Khachiya, Nehemiah, and Kleine's eyes hurt as if they were in danger of cracking. Everybody stops. It is the child, singing a note of power that weaves around the jailer, surrounding him in a green phosphorescent circle. The circle looks vaguely like a paramecium and lifts him in the air, suspended, floating above all of them.

"You can't do that!" screams Glenn. "He's been hurting us for decades." Is it petty to point out that the jailer has only been hurting Glenn himself for the past couple of years? But in fact all the prisoners are looking at the child with the most profound look of disappointment, so intense it might be actual depression. How can they not get to hit him?

Yet the child, quiet, just walks forward into the corridor past them all.

"Don't you want to get free?" Kleine asks the dirty people. "I doubt you'll have a chance like this again."

Grumbling and cursing, they follow her and the child. The jailer, in his nimbus, floats above.

∼

The unhoused brother and sister, still crawling on their bellies, pause when they reach the sidewalk in front of the old bank. They are interested, but not astonished, when they see a horse and two llamas standing directly above them.

"Look at them, they're superb," whispers the brother, called Hans. "They really do add to the carnival atmosphere of what we're trying to accomplish!"

Running lightly between the animals, they crawl up the small flight of stairs to the entrance, whereupon they finally get to their feet and look back down the street behind them. Hans and his sister, who goes by Spliffy, expected to see thousands of followers at their back, prepared to rush the jail. Each thought they had a legion of fans behind them as they were crawling.

But no one else is there.

"Wow," Spliffy says dryly. "This isn't how I imagined it."

"Maybe we just make a big speech now and claim victory?"

"Not doing that," she wheezes.

"You're really going in?"

"You're not?"

"I'm going anywhere you're going!" And Hans grips her veiny hand in his and bending, kisses her firmly on the head.

They walk forward the one or two steps remaining to the bank's huge door. As they prepare to enter, they are, finally, surprised to feel something animal and wet on the back of their heads. It is a horse's soft muzzle.

∼

Inside, the harlequin feels the vampires sucking his love away. Sucking away his commitment to the good, his juiciness, even his strong natural passion that "comes native with the warmth" inside him, all of it draining slowly into their mouths, their huggy anuses, their squeezy hands.

He remembers. When it happened before.

Not vampires but . . . flowers? Or a person who was like a bunch of flowers.

Draining him. Taking him away. All of him. She was mad when he kept even a little in reserve, apart, for himself.

"You have no self."

∼

A blue wasp, sitting on a vampire's shoulders, whispers to the harlequin, "You have to get out of here."

In that moment he's afraid of acknowledging that a wasp is talking to him, so he pretends that he said it himself.

And responds: "There is no way out."

"There has to be."

"How can I get away from them?"

"You have a gift for lying and beguilement, freak. Use it!"

As soon as he hears this, the harlequin opens his arms as far as he can. Gulps in scared breaths, and begins painting images on the air for the vampires to see: Vast scenes of ruddy-faced people fucking and sucking. Round apricot-color titties, red glowing labia like opened fruit, pretty purple penises waving. The vampires arise from their stupor of kissing Bobby, of sucking him in everywhere, and begin attacking the fake people in the air.

The harlequin crashes out the door and into the giant bank lobby.

∽

The harlequin's trick, Hylas, says, "What am I supposed to do now?"

The hairy naked man says, "Just be, sweetheart. Just keep looking as fabulous as you do now."

"I want to go home."

"You ARE home."

Hylas pauses for just three seconds to think. Then he clubs the beautiful naked man over the head with the water jug and runs out of the apartment like a bullet.

∽

The four prisoners, led by the jailer floating in his cloud and the child walking close behind him, meander down the hallway. Khachiya, Glenn, Nehemiah and Sloppy make their footfalls heavy, peevish, like teenagers. They clomp, Nehemiah flinging spitballs made of shit into the rooms as they pass them. Kleine listens to their surprisingly non-happy talk as she brings up the rear.

"I don't get it," she tells them. "Why aren't you guys thrilled? You've been liberated."

"Number One," Sloppy says, "We're not out of here yet. Number Two, you haven't liberated us. I got out of my own cell and I freed the rest. Number Three, why should we be happy?"

Kleine's face clouds over. Why should they be happy? They've lived here for years. She herself feels depressed and scared, and she's only been inside the jail one hour.

～

In the lobby, the harlequin feels a rush of joy at the sight of Falhófnir, but who are those cute Goth homeless people rubbing the horse's flanks? "Hey!" he says. "I'm the harlequin."

"We've heard of you!" Hans whispers smilingly, cruising him.

"I think I may have heard of you, too."

"We try to keep a low profile," Spliffy says, "but word does tend to get around because nobody else resists very much in this city."

The harlequin's feelings are hurt. *He* resists—in fact, he's been a radiant force of liberation his whole life! He has to clamp his lips shut to refrain from telling them, "*I'm* legendary!"

Falhófnir snorts.

"We've come here to break the prison and free people," Spliffy says. "Want to help?"

"We've already freed the child," says Bobby a little snidely. "But we still need to get the other, ah, prisoners, and I have to find my comrade Kleine. We got separated—"

"Time's a-wasting," Hans says. "Let's stop holding back from the action, and go in there." Bobby quickly works a spell so that they can all see the sideways door, but Hans and Spliffy just walk through it without noticing or caring that he did anything special. Bobby feels an old hurt opening up inside him but there is Falhófnir in the doorway behind him, nuzzling his hair.

∼

The jailer wakes up floating through the air in a cloudy green oval. He is horizontal, like Adam or God in the Michelangelo painting, seeping through the hallways above the child, who plods directly below in Bobby's silk shirt.

The jailer is in pain all over. He's pretty sure his knees are not going to work anymore, and his balls hurt so much he understands, finally, why some prisoners would rather die than be electroshocked there. His life energy, such as it is, seems to be seeping out his neck through two little holes that weren't there before.

Oh no. If he gives any indication he'll accept this, it's all over. He calls down to the child: "Dumbass! You forgot to fix my pain."

The child, and the whole procession behind her, come to an abrupt stop. She blushes immediately. "I'm sorry, Daddy."

"You haven't done anything to him!" Kleine blurts, furious. "He should stop speaking to you like that!"

"Fuck you too, dumbass!" the jailer spits in Kleine's direction. "She's supposed to fix everything. If you don't like what I'm doing to the kid, you should wait to see what I'm going to do to you!"

The child sits down on the musty floor and starts crying.

"That's enough!" Kleine tells the jailer, her voice gone low and cold.

"Honey," she says to the little girl, "is there a way you can make it so none of us can hear what your daddy is saying in that little cloud? And so you can't hear it either? Just temporarily, while we walk out of this building. I promise you'll be able to hear and talk to him later if you want. Can you do that for me?"

"I'm very confused!" screams the girl at all of them. "You're all telling me to do different things. Plus, Daddy hates me!" Her face has gone bright red, and deep bags can suddenly be seen beneath her child's eyes. She takes off running down the corridor before anyone can think to catch her.

∼

Much later that evening, the divine mother shows up unannounced at Anna and Frank's apartment. "You have a gentlewoman caller!" Frank sings out happily.

Anna comes out in a crusty sweatshirt and stained pajamas. She's been crying.

"What can possibly be wrong, my love?" Magna asks her.

"He's getting worse. I can tell."

"I can, too." Magna frowns. "Funny, we both know exactly who we're talking about, and we both know exactly how he's doing. You from 30 blocks away, and me from 100 miles up! And oh yeah, I'm just as sad about it! Do you have any ice cream?"

"We have a lot of ice cream, honey!" Frank, sympathetic, is already at the freezer door. "Pumpkin mascarpone, triple-dark chocolate caramel. . . ."

Anna interrupts, eyeing Magna. "I was hoping maybe you'd take me out instead?"

The goddess smiles and recalibrates, changing her own clothes with a single gesture of her fingers, from the denim of her workshop to a midnight-black velvet tuxedo.

∼

Earlier that afternoon, Hylas, running in his fashionable dress, bumps his knee on a fire hydrant in the fancy neighborhood.

"Easy there! Nice outfit!" says Mala, out on a mission to secure the donation of a hammer and some screwdrivers.

"Thanks," he says. He doesn't know whether to stop to ask for help or keep running. He keeps looking around to watch the street, then turning back to her, dizzyingly. He is scared. "I'm kind of, I have a problem, and I need to get out of these clothes. Do you know anywhere I could get some used clothes, cheap?"

"I'm the perfect person for that."

And in 15 minutes they have zigzagged down five alleys to evade pursuers, and arrived at Mala's encampment.

∼

Five officers awaken in the station room. "Something's not right," says Pepowitz, a little bit of donut falling from his mouth. "Someone's been in the cage room who shouldn't have been." He can tell by the smell.

Gray is annoyed. "Who cares? We're going to flush the little brat down the toilet. We're going to do it right now, get up!"

"Lemme just get this last coconut cruller, chief," Smith pipes up.

"No!" Gray bats his hand away from the box. "We're going now." Groans all around from men who want one final snack to bear them up before the action starts.

The lieutenant takes a curious device from his desk that looks like a pen-sized baseball bat, and points it at the grease stain on the piss yellow wall. A tiny hole opens and Gray and Pepowitz, followed by Rathbaum, Anxious, and Smith muttering and cursing behind them, stagger through.

It reeks in the hamster room, and they can see dirty piles of straw in the center. But there is no one there.

"Something bad," says Anxious. "A bad thing is happening to us."

"No shit, Sherlock," says the lieutenant.

∼

Magna has taken Anna to the Starlight Ballroom, one of the finest places in Donnaville. The stars are glittering through a ceiling made completely of glass. The ballroom underneath is mostly dark. A masculine woman maître d' in a fitted black suit takes their jackets, leads them to banquettes and a table with a plate of elegant, crispy cheese straws.

"What do you like to drink, Magna?"

"Me? I can't drink alcohol anymore, but if you buy me a drink I can bewitch the alcohol out of it but keep the high it induces. I have a special trick no one knows," the divine mother winks.

"Waiter! Champagne for two!"

The champagne in their glasses twinkles. They get up to dance.

Anna's face, neck, and breasts are rosy, swelling up from her dress. Magna touches her cheek, which is warm as a little bird. They are dancing fast then slow under the open ceiling, in the shimmery dark. Their hips and shoulders bump softly, and soon they are just a protected circle, a glittery bubble of sorts bouncing around together over the floor.

"Look. You can see the whole city from here."

"This city doesn't look any nicer from anywhere than from right here, right now."

CHAPTER 8

Through the sideways door from the bank, Bobby, Falhófnir, Hans and Spliffy arrive in the station room. No one is there. But in an instant, the five guards have returned through the tiny hole in the wall, with cries of glee as they fall on the intruders. Falhófnir surges up and kicks Smith and Pepowitz in the chest. Bites Lieutenant Gray in the head.

Anxious sprints back through the piss-hole, but Rathbaum seizes Bobby around the neck and presses the point of a great knife to his throat. "Look what I've found! He's supposed to be an old wives' tale, but the Evil Harlequin exists and I've got his half-naked little faggoty body in my hands." As he begins sticking the fine tip ever so slightly into Bobby's neck, Spliffy doesn't think twice. She launches herself at Rathbaum's head and somehow winds up impaled on the man's teeth.

∼

The child is running through corridors. A huge black spider, dangling from a thread as long as a human being, lands on her face. It sits on her nostrils so her breath is stopped. She screams, squirming it off of her, and runs all the way down a series of L-shaped halls until she gets to the bank lobby. She runs straight through the bank and out the two high doors, into the street.

∽

"She's eight years old!" Bobby says. "What you mean you lost her?"

"She got very upset when the others started hurting the jailer. I did my best," says Kleine defensively.

"I should have done this by myself."

"Yeah, no. You couldn't have done it yourself, asshole. You needed me to bring the jailer out and get the other prisoners."\

Hans makes a scratchy noise in his throat. "Will you two please stop fighting? We are all in danger and we have to keep everyone safe, NOW!"

His sister is stretched out on one of the old bank's check-writing tables, gashed with three thick cuts in her face that the harlequin stanched with horsehair.

"Yeah, that's definitely the job of all you heroes, keeping us safe," sniffs Khachiya. She's clustered, with her three ex-prisoner compatriots, around the large black-leather-and-walnut desk of the bank director, which they have seized as their home base.

At the other end of the bank, as far away from them as possible, the jailer floats near the ceiling, tapping on a mural that depicts the rise of the money economy. Green dollar bills with arms, legs, and wings fly from the hands of nobles into artisans' purses. Soon, the dollars fly smiling around factories, sailing into workers' pockets to be exchanged for live, red chickens and loaves of bread at bustling markets. The chickens, also smiling, fly into pots in the laborers' kitchens.

Falhófnir neighs loudly, then looks daggers at all of them. He means it's time to leave.

Bobby, grumbling under his breath, and Kleine, growling,

work together without looking at each other. Taking each of the wounded guards by head and feet, they drag them outside. Hans holds the massive doors open for them.

"We don't want to leave!" Nehemiah and Glenn announce in unison to the resisters. "We like it here."

"But there's no food inside the prison," whispers Hans.

Glenn gives him a complicated stare. "None of your business, rent boy. But if you really care, you should be able to figure out that we can squat in here and go out for dinner whenever we like."

∿

"I was hoping we could just burn the place down."

"No chance of that now."

The harlequin and Kleine, reconciled minutes ago, are talking in low voices around a campfire.

"I have the distinct feeling that the jail is not supposed to be there," Bobby says.

"No, it's not. But that jail got built anyhow, almost 50 years ago, and it's been here ever since."

"What would happen if we just forced the inmates out? Like, if we pushed them out and then lit a match quickly to the place?"

"I don't really want to go there, to use violence against people who've already been so violated, do you?"

∿

Nehemiah, Khachiya, Glenn, and Sloppy go out for dinner. Their strategy for getting it without money is to enter restaurants by the back door, where the kitchen is. They immediately show themselves to the cooks—Nehemiah still covered with shit, and the rest, except for Sloppy, still stinking and covered with dirt. The cooks all flee, so the four of them can seize whole cooked chickens, plates of pommes frites, all kinds of baked, glazed vegetables they have never tried. Deliciousness.

"Sweet," says Khachiya.

From a counter, Sloppy grabs a few bottles of wine and a corkscrew.

"What's that thing for, man?" chortles Nehemiah, grabbing one of the bottles and smashing the top against a parking meter. He pours purple wine into his mouth from the broken tip.

∼

The vampires are still around. Perhaps the jailbreakers just forgot about them? The jail is not the suckers' native habitat, after all. They live elsewhere in Donnaville, haunting the parks at evening, basements, rivers, caves. But they're in the prison now. In the night, the three undead stalk the ex-prisoners who are camped out grandly on the well-constructed desks of the bank director, the associate director, and the desk reserved for Very High Net Worth individuals.

The four ex-inmates have been sleeping right next to one another, so the vampires must wait for one or another of them to get up to go to the bathroom. For some reason, the ex-inmates will only go in the actual prison.

Alternatively, they must wait for them to return to the prison with some other kind of urge. Some of the four ex-prisoners return to pace, over and over, past the cells they lived in for years. Some of them actually go back inside their cells, shut the door and pretend they still are forced to be on those stinking floors waiting for the jailer to come. And they shake, shake for the entire night.

∼

A few hours earlier:

The child, still wearing Bobby's purple silk shirt as a kind of tunic or dress, walks through the streets in wonder. It is still daylight, and office workers are strolling, enjoying the beauty of the late afternoon sun on the old office buildings, the storefronts, the little trees planted only recently in the business district. The girl is amazed at the golden light.

Inside a Staples, there is a water fountain and she drinks for a long time. There is vomit on her feet from her long run through the jail and she tries to wash it off in the Staples bathroom but she is new to washing and there are some green bits left.

∼

Before the prisonbreaking comrades left the scene, Spliffy had looked up at the green cloud still enclosing the jailer like an amniotic sac and said:

"We have to do something about that. We can't just let him stay in there."

"Yeah, but how can we protect people from him otherwise?" said Kleine.

Bobby said plaintively, "He's not gonna grow unless we break him out of that thing."

Hans said, "I have no idea how you expect to do that safely. Anyhow, some of *our* friends want to stab him."

Bobby drew himself up to his full height then and said as earnestly as he knew how, "I know he has to survive, and he can't just be ignored or walled off. I don't know how I know that, but it's true."

They had all grabbed around them then for long metal poles, the kind you use to prop up gates on stores. There were some by the bank, and by the Staples and a paperstand nearby. They also grabbed a metal trash can or two. Then they all attacked the cloud like a piñata, and as it broke, the jailer fell to earth like a big piece of candy, landing safely in a dumpster full of sand.

∾

Khachiya and Sloppy are playing a game in Sloppy's old cell. "Now YOU be the jailer and come in and hit me!"

"Sloppy, you're a little turd!" Khachiya says in the jailer's creepy cellar voice, hitting her friend about the shoulders and head.

Sloppy reaches out a long leg and trips her.

"Dude, what the fuck?" Angry, she grabs his balls and twists hard. Now they are fighting in earnest.

∾

The jailer notices that he's been deposited in sand, in what appears to be a giant cat litter box.

He feels immediately the child's absence—she is out of the prison.

Beyond his reach.

How many times has he abandoned her? And now he has

done nothing to stop her from leaving. He touches the side of his lip as he always does when uncertain and close to despair. He is supposed to make her better. That's his job. He is supposed to guide her and teach her, show her who to be and how to live.

She's his charge. He thinks of her running naked with her feelings through the streets, vulnerable, rosy, feeling everything, and he thinks of how deep inside, inside the vast tenderness inside her, she'll be hurt, and it's unbearable.

∼

Anna wakes in Magna's bed, having experienced the best thing she has ever known. She felt fully safe and warm. She felt fully known.

She gently gropes the blanket next to her, but Magna isn't there.

Where did she go? Peculiarly, the room has no door. There are windows, but she tries and is unable to open them. She tries throwing her shoes through them, but they apparently can't be broken, either. There is no way for her to get out. Far, far up on the 20-foot ceiling is an open skylight, but even if she somehow manages to stack the dresser on top of the bed, it is too high for her to ever climb up out of there. How could Magna lock her in and leave her?

∼

As for the divine mother, right now she is running very quickly down the street 100 miles beneath her heavenly villa, sprinting through the city of Donnaville to get to the jailer.

She finds him, still in the cat-litter dumpster, weeping.

"Mr. Jailer," she says.

"Don't call me that. I haven't been worthy of that name for a long time. I keep nothing safe. I keep nothing protected."

She climbs up the dumpster and sits down with him in the sand. "Maybe that was never what you were supposed to do. Maybe what you're really good at is something else." She pats his arm.

"Oh, that's bullshit," says the jailer. "We both know that what I'm really good at is torturing."

∽

In the mountains south of the city, Spliffy and Hans have joined Kleine and the harlequin around the campfire. Kleine built the fire from the fallen chestnut wood all over the clearing.

All of them are thrilled to be out in the fresh air of late March, wildflowers of all colors poking up through the soil of the mountain, the stars all visible and the moon huge as they go off to bed.

The harlequin has supplied everyone with clean sleeping bags, extra blankets and filled water bottles, but he hasn't told anyone where he got these things. Mysteriously, some peanut butter and jelly sandwiches wrapped in tinfoil have also turned up by the campfire—but not even the harlequin knows where they came from.

Hans and Spliffy have taken their sleeping bundles a little ways away, and they are whispering together as the owls call.

"We don't usually work with folk like this," Spliff says. "What if they have some agenda we don't know about?"

"They may be bourgie, but they both seem pretty cool."

"We have to resist the lure of new equipment and certain cute idealistic types who never spent a night on the street."

"Dude, they got the child out. They got everybody out. They joined with us to take out the guards."

"It's fishy. How were they able to do all those things?"

∽

As the night progresses, the harlequin sits alone on the slightly damp ground and wonders if Hylas is still alive.

I had to pick the little girl. It is agony, but if we don't defend children, who are we? She was going to be flushed away. Hylas is an adult.

∽

The child has suddenly become aware of how much she smells, despite washing in the Staples bathroom. People move away from her in the park, on crowded streets.

I'm lonely. People don't like me. I smell like a hamster cage.

But hunger drives her. She identifies with the animals she sees, the pigeons and the park rats, as she scavenges for pieces of abandoned sandwiches and fruit. Perhaps she can build a house out of what other people throw away, out of orange peels and plastic water bottles, walnut shells and sailing yogurt lids.

∽

Hylas is shaking uncontrollably. "What's wrong with this city, anyway?"

Mala purses her lips. She's not great at comforting people, but she feels bad for this stranger who keeps turning around to see whether someone is coming to hurt him. "We're not such a great place, it's true. We can be a scary place to be stuck in."

"But I met the nicest guy here. A sweet *sweet* personality, and he could be really tender—"

They are in Mala's storage-unit compound, and she is mopping the sweat off his arms and looking him over for any cuts or puncture wounds she needs to treat. She paints his shallow wounds with iodine. She understands suddenly. "He CAN be a very sweet boy."

∽

"Why are you always running to take care of my father?" The child is furious, shaking her hands up at the sky. "Why don't you look after me?"

A dirty rain falls on her.

Somebody is listening, hears her.

∽

"I think I should leave you on your own for a bit," the divine mother tells the character who used to be known as the jailer. "I think maybe you should take care of yourself for a while."

"Fucking bitch!" says the jailer. "How dare you?"

∽

At the campground in the mountains, Kleine is up early, grilling fish she caught. A few moments ago, she built the grill herself with some rocks.

The smell wakes the harlequin. "I love fish!" He kisses her cheek with enthusiasm, starts to say "Now, if we only had coffee—" But he abruptly shuts himself up.

"When are you going to stop holding out on me?" Kleine cries, playfully pummeling his arms. "I know you have a secret place near here!" She kisses his cheek and head.

He tries to look dumb. Can't quite manage it, so he winks. "Yeah, coffee would be AMAZING right now, don't you think? If only we had ourselves some!"

"You nincompoop!"

"My home is here, just behind those trees." He's never told a single person about his nut before. "I'm pretty sure I have a fancy coffeemaker in there, but not a single bag of coffee."

"No coffee?" She's incredulous. "You seem like someone who would love good coffee. Why don't you have any?"

"Yeah, I'm pretty weird that way," he smiles ruefully, "I don't often supply myself with a lot of things that I love."

∼

The vampires are interested in the child. Her inner nature draws them, smelling of bergamot.

In fact, the child would be pretty easy to find at this moment if the vampires could rip themselves away from the blood sources much closer to them. The girl is in an open meadow in the large park in the north central west of Donnaville. There, in a garbage can near the playground, she finds a foil sack with a coating of Cheeto dust, and a baggie with some funky carrot sticks. She fights a pigeon for a whole half of an abandoned meatball hero and wins, using her torn-off shirt to strike against its beak.

Some of the park moms take in her physical stink and bare feet, and dive for their phones to call social services. But one of their friends, an artist mom with messy hair and slightly stained clothes, wards them off, a finger on her lips. She walks over to the child very slowly, like an experienced conservation veterinarian approaching a wolf. Stopping three feet away, she faces the girl and shouts, "DO YOU HAVE A MOMMY?"

The child runs. She avoids playgrounds after that when people are in them. But late that night, she washes herself and her shirt in the abandoned plaza fountain using a bar of soap she stole from the chambermaid's cart at the midtown Days Inn. She still looks funny, and the silk shirt takes many days to dry, but she doesn't smell anymore.

∼

The child consults a map she stole from a convenience store. According to the laminated, brightly colored tourist map, on the western edge of Donnaville there is a wild area called Rubus Fruticosus covered with blackberry vines and rosebushes.

"Few visit Rubus because of the razor-sharp thorns in the bramble." The child thinks it sounds promising. She could eat the blackberries and nobody would bother her. She wants to eat berries, and to see a rose.

∼

The jailer is sitting in the street on the the unofficial border between midtown and downtown, begging. Since Magna left him in the dumpster, none of her sandwiches have appeared at regular intervals like they used to. She'd been feeding him ever since he'd stopped working at the jail. He'd grown particularly fond of the chopped liver with raw onion and the deli-style tuna with lots of mayonnaise and celery.

Now the bitch hasn't left him a sandwich in over a day, and he feels ravenous in a way he never felt at the jail. Before he met her, all he ever took in was the milk that hurt him. And because of that bitch, last week he had started once again craving and eating real food, beautiful honey cakes, bread that had been baked that morning, and the Italian lady's ragu.

∼

If the child is reading the map correctly, it will take her three days to reach the western marches of Donnaville. With her short legs, she can't walk more than two miles a day, even if she can figure out which direction to walk and where to find food and drink nearby. She's counting on dumpster diving the first day outside Key Food, but she won't get there till nightfall. What will she eat in the meantime?

∼

The goddess returns to her radiant bedroom, remembering last night, a sacred interchange whose meaning is still growing inside her. But gliding down into her room on the wind of delightful memory, she sees that her lover is gone. How did the human woman get away?

"That's just not possible!" Magna growls to herself, frustrated. To get into the goddess's fortress or out of it, you need to fly.

"Sensuality! Delight! Falhófnir!" She knows the llamas at least would have returned from jailbreaking by now.

Sensuality comes bounding up.

"Where is the woman?"

Sensuality bats her eyelashes, gives the goddess to understand that Delight flew down and took the beautiful human woman all the way home.

"Fuck!"

∼

Anna feels shaky after her night with the goddess.

In one way, it was the best night of her life.

But in another—what kind of monster leaves you locked inside their bedroom, unable to get away?

She's just lucky that the llama flew in through the skylight, offering his broad back for flight.

Anna is sad, she's full of longing, and she mourns.

∼

Mala is worried about her charges, the other people who live in and around her storage units. Many are ill, and these days it's not so easy to find food for free. Both the McDonald's with its ever-full dumpster and the Tasty Bread outlet have shut down in the past few days. The one actual farm in Donnaville, the one that lies out toward the east, does not allow people to glean its leavings anymore.

On the other hand, Hylas makes an excellent addition to the storage-unit community. He's handy with a hammer and saw, and he can sing. Late at night when Mala and the 20 or so other residents are sitting around the bonfire they have laid in a garbage can, he teaches them songs from Upper Caspia, some of the other residents accompanying him on guitars, mandolins, and harps handmade from dental floss and bits of wood.

Tonight, everyone is around the fire singing. Many are coughing, in between taking handfuls of popcorn Mala made for them in her own storage unit, where she has an Orville Redenbacher.

Hylas is sitting near her, chomping on the delicious yellow stuff, when a look of longing comes into his eyes. "Bobby," he says slowly, "I think I really ought to go out to look for Bobby."

∾

The harlequin is showing Kleine around his nut. This is a first in the history of the harlequin, and of Donnaville.

This is how he shows her around: they both stand outside, and he opens first one panel, then another to show her the interior. It is black, compact, and very punky.

"Well, it is sexy looking," she says. "But where's all the food and drink at? Or the bathroom?"

He mockingly hangs his head.

"I have been pretty strangely abstemious . . . bathroom's outside, and I never used to eat much till recently."

"I don't even see how you could comfortably fit another

person inside here with you, when you, you know, want to fraternize."

"Yeah, I usually like to go to the other party's place instead." He avoids her eyes.

"Oh yeah," she says. "Me too. But it's nice to have your actual home as a backup, especially if it turns out you like the person!"

∼

E. walks to the art gallery to meet Donna, who is supposed to speak at an art opening by visual artists. Donna, who can't paint or draw, has wangled herself a role in the program by offering to read a piece of writing on the exhibition's theme, HAIRPIECES. She doesn't have a hairpiece either, but it will work if she uses hairpieces as a metaphor for gender.

E. texts Donna the emoji for "ham." Below, she writes, "U R a juicy ham."

Donna writes back: "I AM a juicy ham."

They enjoy an enormous, luscious smoked ham sandwich together after the opening, dabbed with the nicest mayonnaise, falling down laughing together on the restaurant table.

∼

The jailer vomits. He has rarely done this so far, is afraid to. He has always been proud that in five decades, he has vomited only twice, each time before the age of 10. He has mastered himself since then. The milk he forced himself to gulp down gave him eczema and frequent diarrhea, but it never made him throw up. "I am in control," he used to say, drinking milk in the mirror.

But this morning he ate a corned beef hash from a dented, open can somebody tossed, and his body is unhappy with him.

The jailer's body: "Why you hurt me all the time, bro?"

He is shocked. The last time his body spoke to him was the last time he made love, in 1994.

The jailer's body: "You're a sweet little dude, and I love you, baby. But why don't you try to treat me nice?"

He screws up his face, confused. He always feels afraid when people tell him that they love him. He decides to get out of this conversation, so he hits his body to get it to shut up. He hits it in the head.

~

Spliffy and Hans have decided to change their base of operations, which they haven't done since 1992. But astonishing themselves, they're not returning to the plaza or its fountain, but are trying out a large tent city of the unhoused in the east of Donnaville. The camp obtrudes into the tourist and entertainment district, mutually influencing and being influenced by the artists there.

These unhoused people are much more involved in the arts than the ones who used to sit and listen to them in the plaza.

In the morning, the tent dwellers tell stories. As everyone sits around drinking bad coffee in a gathering spot that folks have set up with rough benches near the water tank, a queer person named Arrow comes out and tells a traditional tale about a god who smothered brilliant beings in a fire to quench their unquenchable light. A woman named Abby brings out her paintings, crazy bright curves and lines and lozenges in colors like fruit and people's bodies.

"Here are some peanut butter and jelly sandwiches we found," Spliffy says, ambivalence clear in her voice. "We honestly have no fucking idea where they came from, but they taste good, and they're on whole wheat."

Their new neighbors reach for the packets, delighted.

∼

The divine mother is writing a letter to Anna.

"I am very sorry," she says. "I did not realize you might feel hampered or angry at not being able to leave, although of course that makes perfect sense. I myself can get out of any enclosure, so I haven't actually thought about what it might be like to have to stay somewhere against your will.

"I hope you can forgive me. I would like to see you again, because being with you changes me in ways I have always wanted to be changed."

∼

Hylas is setting out on his long road to find the harlequin. Mala is worried, so she has outfitted him with a wooden sword, a wooden shield, and a sack of hard-boiled eggs, which constitutes a treasure among the storage-container folk.

"You really have been kind to me," he says, looking at her wonderingly.

"No sweat, honey," she says, embarrassed. "Just remember to send me a wedding invitation."

She gives him, too, a map she copied from one on her own wall. Both are odd. The one on her wall is painted in beautiful dark-blue brushstrokes, and comprises mountains indicated at the bottom with inverted v's, a strange heavy black line leading from nowhere to nowhere in the east, and vines drawn by hand across the western edge, as in an illustration for a gardening book. In the middle, more or less, are a few bare red dots.

The map she copied out for him contains a few scraps of additional information. "I would look here for the harlequin," she has written in her uncharacteristically pretty cursive hand along the mountains at the bottom.

"Who is the harlequin?" he asks.

She goes completely still for a moment. He doesn't know. "He's your—What name did you use for him? Your lover, your boyf—"

"What's a harlequin?"

∽

The child's legs and stomach hurt. She is not used to walking more than the length and width of the hamster room, which was a rough oval with a diameter of about 12 feet. Now night is falling and she is wondering how to climb up into the tall dumpster outside Key Food. While she considers what to stand on, a man darts out of an SUV and grabs her, but she kicks and bites him until, screaming in pain, he has to set her down. His blood drips on her from where she bit him in the stomach.

She runs at full tilt into the store, not stopping until she is underneath the wheeled tables of pears, apples, and persimmons in the produce section.

∽

"A harlequin is, well, a particular kind of person. Someone extremely tricksy and beguiling—"

"What?"

"The name comes from an old French term meaning King of Hell," Mala adds helpfully.

"WHAT?"

"The harlequin is one of the gods in Donnaville. Well, I don't know if he still is a god, he seemed very vulnerable lately. . . ."

"What are you talking about?" Hylas looks at her unkindly for the first time. He also looks as though he's just swallowed a frog. "Bobby is someone I dated."

∼

Anna reads the letter. She's still mad. She thrusts herself from bed into the kitchen, and wordlessly makes tiny pancakes for herself and Frank.

"How's Your Father's Oldsmobile?" he asks.

"Everything is terrible," she says. She makes their pancakes in the form of little abstracted jail cells, with bars going down the middle.

∼

The harlequin and Kleine are talking long into the night. They can't both fit inside the nut, so Bobby has erected a little lean-to against its side where Kleine, who runs cold, can sleep warm and comfortable in a sleeping bag with a space blanket laid out on top. They sit on her sleeping bag together, passing a bottle of cordial Bobby found by feeling around blindly one night inside one of the nut's most intimate cabinets.

The nut has a lot of obscure internal cabinets, fitted together like those on a ship. He's still not sure what all is in the many cunning layers of his home, arranged for security and compactness long ago.

"Where were you born?" he asks the lean young woman who, except for her practical manner, might be his sister. They even look alike, and have the same air of fearlessness born of early terror.

"I grew up in Donnaville," Kleine says. "I've always lived here, in a sex-crazy hole in the ground on the eastern end. I finally came out and started looking for sex, instead of humping the ground and going insane."

"You're a bit younger than me."

"A few years."

"And you seem to want sex even more than I do."

"I don't know exactly how much you want sex."

"Oh, I want sex! I want sex! I was, um, very surprised though when I found myself touching the goddess. She's not my, ah, usual type but when I touched her it was like brushing up against the electrical source of all life."

CHAPTER 9

The electrical source of all life is at this very moment laid out in bed in a spare room (because being in the bed she shared with Anna would be unbearable now). She has a migraine, which is particularly acute because the shades on all the goddess's windows—where there even are shades—are irredeemably light. They're little gossamer scraps meant to provide privacy for her guests, not shut out the sun. Normally, she loves sunlight. She has never been in a situation like this, where her beautiful, bursting friend the sun, whose rays taste like sweet fruit juice, apricot, mango, to her, hurts her. Is suddenly an enemy.

She rises, shakes herself from head to toe, takes a huge swig of seltzer from the refrigerator and goes down, down, down stairs upon stairs into the true ground of her house, the foundation of her fortress, the dark room. Not a photography room but a room of darkness, the empty room, where failure is possible and death can happen even to immortals. The source room.

The room has always been there and it's finally time for her to enter it.

∼

Under the persimmon table in Key Food, the child meets a rat. It is beautiful, so she reaches out to stroke the soft brown fur but the rat is alarmed and snaps its giant teeth at her.

The child escapes to the frozen section, where she calms herself by breathing in, breathing out very very carefully, until she no longer wants to beat her fists against the peas and scream as loud and high-pitched as she possibly can. She grabs a frozen burrito, sticks it under her purple shirt, and with its comforting painful freeze against her belly, slowly, walking like a competent block of ice, makes it to the exit.

∽

People leave the jailer alone as he hits himself in the park. There is vomit on his nice leather shirt, and his silky but masculine black pants no longer look either silky or masculine, stained as they are with bird shit, dust, and tears.

He cries a lot now. He's hungry.

He no longer has any will to restrict himself to milk, but it's hard to find food of any kind that doesn't make him sick.

The Park Slope playground mothers notice him and decide he's not a threat, but don't call social services. Actually, the social services in Donnaville stopped working long ago, if they were ever truly operative. Donnaville's social services have been limited to bad foster care and terrible criminal justice for a very long time.

∽

In a two-family house in the nice neighborhood by the river, Donna watches TV. She's been enjoying a show about women cops who are buddies and secretly love one another. Then, because it is a beautiful day, she gets up and opens the back door to see the mountains behind her house, the grass in the backyard, the battered blue picnic table where she now sits, watching the sky.

She eats a piece of toast with hummus and pickles at the picnic table. She goes upstairs to write. She pays no attention to any of the 32,000 other people in Donnaville, who live mainly in the other neighborhoods. Her life is great! But in her dreams every night, a child freezes itself so it will be able to walk to its next destination without crying out and an old man weeps in the park, blubbering, so loud that gangs of young toughs slip out of the bushes to hurt him enough to shut him up.

∼

Khachiya has a black eye and Sloppy is bleeding from his face and arms when the vampires come in the cell where the ex-prisoners have been "playing."

The three vampires, in their tight black T-shirts and jeans, eat both of them up.

∼

Glenn, on a 3 AM pee walk to the prison, looks in Sloppy's old cell and sees nothing but blood on the floor.

He makes his feet slow. Slow. And silent. *Very silent.* He walks lightly back through the bloodstained corridor, and walks backward steadily through the sideways door.

"What's goin' on, dude?" Nehemiah cocks a sleepy eye at him.

Glenn smiles. "Need a cigarette," he stage-whispers, and is out on little cat feet through the huge ebony doors of the bank. Once his long body has made it through the door, he runs.

∽

"I'm not sure about a few things that we appear to have left undone," Kleine says.

"The other prisoners?"

"Not just them, sheesh. *The guards.*"

Bobby grimaces. "What more were we supposed to do? We stopped them from being guards."

"No. We stopped them from being guards *in the prison*. What's to stop them from acting like guards in the street, say? To all the other people in Donnaville?"

"Wow, look at you, you're really kind of smart, aren't you?" He looks at her with the kind of toothy smile he usually reserves for an elite group of the cutest boys. But it's not that he wants to take Kleine to bed, he just . . . is delighted by her. And wants to do a number on her.

"Hey, stop charming me." But she likes it. Not enough people ever flirt with Kleine, just as not enough people ever tell Bobby that he's legendary.

"No, you're a smart cookie. And practical. I normally can only do things that come from my natural magic, you know, from my intrinsic self. But you, you actually figure out how to *do stuff.*"

"I haven't figured out how to do anything about the jailer's minions. Or about that kid, she's all alone in this city and she's only eight."

"How can you be so practical when you're even more insecure than I am?"

Anna's fried pies have been—not to put too fine a point on it—tasting like shit. Either they're burnt and black, or she doesn't get the oil hot enough and they're greasy and gross. She hates to sell food that is so bad, but the truth is that the tourists will buy them anyway and she needs the money.

She simply doesn't earn that much from handheld fried apple pies to begin with. The margins for her life's passion are small.

Tourists are besotted with the city, though. They'll buy anything. Anna's face itself has begun to look as greasy as her pies, pimpled, disaffected. Frank has noticed because Anna is normally so attractive. In fact, although she's not a boy, she's usually the most gorgeous and alive-looking individual he sees all day. She wears a belt with a big silver buckle, her short hair is jet black, and her skin is olive. She shows a fair amount of skin, but she's at least part butch. With enough studs on her clothes to be punk as fuck.

"C'mon, sweetie," he says, "you're coming out on the town with me tonight. C'mon. You are."

"Aw, I don't feel like it, Frankie."

"All those lesbians, deprived of your cute *punim* for so long, I can't stand it. That's enough, you're coming with me."

Kleine gives the harlequin a manifold look—clearsighted, guarded, interested, vulnerable, and bold.

"Well, I AM insecure, but that doesn't mean I want to talk with you about it right now."

"Because you're insecure."

"Okay." She stops, stops completely all of a sudden, and draws herself up to her full height of 5 foot two. For an instant he can see burning light coming off the top of her head, not the corrosive burn of rage but the fire of power. "I SAID we weren't going to talk about it right now. If you keep pushing me this way, you aren't going to like the result."

∿

In the dark room, there are enormous metal hooks hanging from the ceiling. Magna steps forward, undaunted, and impales herself on the largest and sharpest radiant hook.

The barbed thing enters at the top of her head, pierces her skull, and continues spiraling down her trunk, bringing horror as it goes. It comes out of her at her *dan tien*, the center of a person's life-energy in Chinese thought—identified as a spot "two or three finger widths" below one's belly button.

The hook is made of starlight, but it feels like any other fishhook in the body.

∿

The child is still walking towards Rubus Fruticosus. It's the second day of her journey toward the bramble. An old sign reading JOE'S LAUNDRY in giant green-gray letters has a friendly look, a roof-mounted billboard opening onto a neighborhood of low buildings and rowhouses. Nearby is a cheap cafeteria selling old-fashioned dishes like meatloaf, chicken and dumplings, ham hock. The child wants a ham hock but she has no money. She enters anyhow, curious, smelling the meat and cream smells, watching elderly customers who play pinochle as they eat.

An old man with thin arms and thin legs motions her to sit. Except for white wisps at the sides of his face he is bald as a cue ball, with a freckled face. "Eat something, *bubele*." He motions to a giant platter on the table he's sharing with three other oldsters: there are blintzes with sour cream, grits with ham hock, roast chicken. "They have everything here!"

"You sure?" she's incredulous.

"Eat," he gestures to the platter.

She selects a ham hock. The two men and two women applaud. One of the women, in a green oversize dress and little orange pumps, passes her a plate. They all ignore their card game to watch her enjoy.

It's the best thing she can ever remember eating. What is that sensation on her tongue, the taste of something incredibly rich and a little fecund, like soil, with a very faint flavor of rot in it, but somehow delicious? And salty. And smoky. She's been given burnt food in the past, but it wasn't like this.

The woman in the oversize dress dishes up some grits onto the child's plate, with a big melty pat of butter in the middle.

"Why are you feeding me?" she wants to know.

"You deserve to be fed!" the other man, wrinkly with dark shaggy hair, winks at her and shakes her hand formally.

∽

At the lesbian bar way downtown, Anna and Frank enter and survey the room.

It's packed tonight—it is a Saturday—and women line the bar and windows, are massed around the pool table so thick that no one can possibly play a round. There are so many gorgeous butches, with newsboy caps and/or short haircuts, red, golden, black, and brown hair, of every race and circumstance, impossibly studly. But there are also femmes with figures that go on for days, with faces that can make you lose your footing. Formfitting dresses that make Anna want to put her arms around their waists and feel their blood beating beneath their vein walls, under the curve.

A short woman, nervous and grumpy, sits at the bar, legs dangling on the barstool because they do not reach the floor. Her hair is butch, blond, and so short that it appears straight, but if you look really closely you can tell it is wavy. There's a cowlick. She grimaces from time to time, and finally, with a great effort of will, orders a rum and Coke from the bartender.

Anna's curious about the short woman on the barstool. All night long, as women come up to Anna and ask her to dance, she scopes the nervous, 5 foot 2 woman at the bar, even as she's jitterbugging with the redhead with the crew cut, dancing close with the woman in purple velvet, pogoing with the butch with short Ghana braids ending in shells.

~

The harlequin is shaky and sad. Has he driven Kleine away for good? He really likes her. Of course, he likes MANY people, that is one of his attributes—to like vast numbers of people, and to be liked by them.

But unlike with all those others, he feels profoundly connected with Kleine. He can tell she understands the deepest parts of him, and there aren't that many people who do and still want him around.

Alone in his nut that seems, suddenly, claustrophobic, he opens a panel, sticks an arm out and feels the breeze on it. He opens five more panels, abruptly steps out of them onto moist earth, and folds the nut away in on itself. For the first time, he puts it away in his pocket. He starts walking, hoping to find her.

∼

Donna's feeling terrible. She was doing fine in her lovely life with her wonderful wife when suddenly she felt her vulnerability all along the entire long, exposed, snakelike surface of the self she extends out into the world.

All the metaphors about this experience are true: She sticks her neck out. She puts herself out there. She takes a leap in the dark. As always, courage fails to keep her safe, and she feels pain all along the pliant surface of her personality as it unfurls, vulnerable as a penis, among all the other human beings in the world. They all have the capacity to hurt her, and some do.

Some fail to appreciate her. Some judge her. Some reject her. Some do none of these things but she fears that they do, or they might.

∼

Magna is hurting, in a different way.

Down on earth, the jailer, lying half on and half off a park bench, suddenly feels her agony, gets a glimpse of it in his mind, hurts inside feeling what that long hook made of starlight feels like, coiled freezing hot and sharp inside her. He can tell that Magna wants the agony to stop but it will not stop, and both of them are surprised, horrified.

In the room at the bottom of her glorious fortress, she feels the jailer hurting for her, and her breath slows. She sees him, far away down in Donnaville, quietly weeping for her, tears seeping out of his rheumy eyes, and she hugs him close with her mental hands.

∼

In the cafeteria, the child is now eating Boston cream pie with whipped cream, while the four old people clap.

She knows their names now. The thin old man's name is Jasper, the voluptuous 75-year-old in the green dress is Cantaloupe, the woman who looks like a bony old scientist is Magreet, and the shaggy guy is Espardenya.

Magreet has blue-black shadows in the crooks of her thin arms and legs and neck, she wears a man's denim shirt with the sleeves rolled up, and she is long and pointy as a billiard cue. "Aren't you a smart one!" she says to the child, grinning with all her teeth. "I bet you're already heading for Rubus Fruticosus."

The child looks at her sharply. "How did you know that?"

"Just guessed. I'm good at guessing, like you!" Magreet's crooked teeth gleam at 45-degree angles to each other, glowing oddly, and the child is frightened.

"Don't mind Magreet," Cantaloupe says, patting the child's arm with her fleshy one. "She *is* a good guesser, and Rubus *is* the most excellent place you could possibly go, and you *are* smart!"

"I am?" asks the child, still very scared.

∼

"So, how's that drink?" Anna asks the short grumpy woman at the bar.

Kleine looks at her, hostile and terrified. She tries looking straight ahead into the mirror behind the bar, then, when she's no longer able to keep that up, turns with an awkward, painful slowness, fakes a smile.

"I think I'll order one too," Anna says with a wide grin. She motions for the bartender.

Kleine does her fake smile/grimace a bit more, then frowns again and looks straight ahead.

"You're not easy, are you?"

"No. I am not easy. But that word can mean different things, and I'm definitely not chaste."

"Oh no, you answered in the sense of easy that I meant."

Kleine turns completely around on her stool and, for the first time, looks Anna completely over.

"So tell me about yourself," she says, looking dead-on into the other's face.

"Well, first thing is, I'm a baker."

"I like food. What do you bake?"

"Special handheld apple pies."

"You got one on you?"

"I do. Is this the moment of truth?"

"Oh, I definitely think so!" says Kleine with a twinkle in her eyes. She's gone completely relaxed. As Anna hands over the pie in its beautiful recyclable wrapping, Kleine tears open the little package and, her eyes never moving from Anna's face, takes a bite.

"Mmmm."

"Like it?"

"It's so juicy!"

"Oh, I don't want it just to be juicy. It has to also have a luxury feel on the tongue, the feel of fat. And you have to taste the cardamom and heat."

"I absolutely have to, huh?"

Anna looks at her shyly.

"Oh, don't worry, baby doll, I do!"

∽

Falhófnir has been off with his lady friend, cavorting in meadows. There has been so much joy in that clover and red clover that I can't even tell you. But one day, feeling the call of sudden need, he rushes off into the entertainment district, where he clocks Hylas through the windows of the fish taco joint. The boy's face is red and he looks strange as he talks to the counterman. As Falhófnir noses his way into the shop, Hylas says sourly, "That taco does not taste like the one I had my first time here. The fish must be rotten."

The 20-year-old counterman looks upset. "It came off the boat this morning."

Hylas takes his long wooden sword off his hip. He points it at the counterman. "I'm not paying for a terrible taco. I want double my money back."

"I can't give you double—"

Before Hylas can use his sword, Falhófnir jumps straight into the space where the boy was standing, through a neat curve he makes in spacetime. Hylas finds himself forced to jump up on the horse's back. His wooden sword and shield clatter to the ground. Falhófnir takes off as though shot from a gun. He doesn't stop until he and Hylas are in the desert, a beautiful place at the eastern end of Donnaville not far from the meadow where he was cavorting with his sweetheart, Greta.

~

Nehemiah wakes in the bank, after a long, delicious sleep. Sunlight streams in through the huge windows on either side of the bank's great hall. He finds himself curiously alone. Not only are the others gone, but somehow he can tell that the remaining bankers' desks have not been slept on. Nor has the check-writing table that Sloppy took for his own bed. It is no matter. He strolls through the sideways door into the prison.

(It looks exactly like a normal door to him, as it does to all who have ever been imprisoned there. They will always be able to return to their cells, as long as the prison stands.)

But this time, Nehemiah just ambles through the warren of corridors till he finds the officers' shower. He takes a long, leisurely, very hot one, washing his body quite free of any rubbed-in shit, and sings loudly, joyously, and operatically in his caramel baritone:

I like my own shit!
But I can also wash it off!
I like my own shit!
But I can also wash it off!
I like my own skin
And I am keeping it NICE!
Skin, I'm washing you with hot water
Because I love you SO!

He is incurious about where his fellow ex-prisoners are, saunters out the front door nonchalantly in search of some breakfast.

Two streets over, he runs into the handsome man who was among those trying to persuade him and his pals to leave the prison.

"HEY-Y-Y!!" he says, clasping the man's muscly forearm in his own.

"Hey, cutie!" says the harlequin, grinning warmly and with a real sweetness.

∽

The jailer wakes surprised on a bench, to full daylight. Both halves of his body are on it, he is glad to see. He doesn't feel that bad; nothing more than a few achy joints and a little acidity in the region of his upper esophagus. His head is clear. It is cloudy and damp out, but considering that, his joints don't ache so much.

There is some $2 whiskey in a lil brown bottle underneath his bench and he drinks it. It goes down well. He stands up and sets off walking.

∽

Jasper and the child are taking a walk through the neighborhood of Joe's Laundry. He brings her into the laundromat, where Joe's niece, Alyia, bends down to say hi. "Alyia just took this place over from Joe," Jasper tells the little girl. "*Sweetaleh*, I thought maybe you two should meet."

The child is taken aback by the young woman touching her arm, but Alyia's smell is alluring, like a campfire mixed with . . . dark fruit? She wants to smell that scent again. (In point of fact, the child has at least a few years of sense-memories that predate the prison.) And "Check this out," the strong-looking, razor-sharp young woman is saying to her, displaying a tattoo of a panther on her shoulder. The child finds the panther surprisingly comforting.

Next, Alyia points to the leather arm-protectors on her muscular forearms. "Do you like these?"

The child is fascinated by the shining black arm-pieces.

"Want to try them on?"

She nods yes, she would like to try them on.

Once they go on her thin arms and are laced up, an amazing change comes over the child. She is taller. Her eyes blaze more.

"There, that's better, isn't it?" says Alyia. "You can keep them if you want!"

The child opens her mouth and says, directly, "Thank you."

Jasper smiles so big that all his laugh lines show. He takes the little girl's hand and they wave goodbye to Alyia.

∽

Afterward, the child spends some time watching the other old man, the one with shaggy black hair, digging in the dirt with his hands.

"Doesn't that hurt?"

"It doesn't hurt," Espardenya tells her, showing her his calluses. "Besides, I touch the soil tenderly, and that is how it touches me back."

They are in his little street garden on the next block over from the laundromat.

"What are you growing?"

"Carrots, artichokes, heart and soul strength."

"Heart and soul strength?"

"Yes," he says, rubbing his long greasy hair. "Heart and soul strength can be grown like any other crop, they just need a *lot* of dead tomatoes in the compost."

"I don't have any dead tomatoes."

"We have a lot and we can give you some."

∼

Meanwhile, in the desert with Falhófnir, Hylas is raging, pacing up and down and yelling first in one direction, then another. "I just want to go home to Upper Caspia! That's all I want. Is that too much to ask!"

Falhófnir looks at him and indicates that Hylas should get on his back.

"But I want to know why I was lovers with a god who is the king of hell!"

Falhófnir looks at him more intently. Rippling his muscles, the horse indicates once again that Hylas should get on his back.

"Yeah, fuck that," says Hylas. He sits down and starts digging in the hot dead-smelling sand, over and over. Dig, dig, dig, dig, dig.

Falhófnir shrugs his massive shoulder.

∼

Nehemiah and Bobby are walking arm in arm. Nehemiah really likes this cat.

"Want to get a beer?"

"Hell yeah!" Nehemiah says, then realizes he can't pull

that sweet stunt with the shit anymore. Don't matter though. They're gonna find a way!

Things are really going good now.

∼

Bobby is wondering how *he* will pay for the beer.

But when they get near the long mahogany bar inside the establishment Bobby chose, the cute curly headed bartender turns in their direction, beaming. His cheeks are bright red. "You're not gonna believe this, boys, it is your lucky day!" He looks high.

Someone has paid for their beers in advance, as many as they need, even the fancy craft kinds if they want.

"Whoa!" Nehemiah says. "I can't stand this amount of luck! You're a cutie PLUS I can drink all the dark and hoppy, creamy things I want to pour inside me!"

∼

Frank left the lesbian bar early and is now snoring loudly. When Anna and Kleine get to the apartment, they try not to make noise but stumble against each other repeatedly trying to find the light, keep going hilariously "Ow! Ow! Ow!"

In Anna's room, Kleine finds a series of red skateboards on the wall and, near the bed, a fantastical ceramic lamp whose base looks like a pie. "Pretty," she says.

"Smell it."

Kleine puts her nose up close to it and, incredibly, the pottery smells not just of apples, but also the hot, high scent of caramelized sugar and the slightly indecent odor of enormous amounts of butter. "How did you do that?"

"I think a lot about flavors and smells."

"But you're not even a potter," Kleine says into her chest.

"I am an apple pie maker," Anna says with satisfaction.

∿

Magna has not slept since she accepted the hook, and she feels it vibrating in her right now, all the way to the tip of the sharp sheer horror coiled inside her. She would not have willed this, had she known. She would not have volunteered for it, had she known. All she can think to do is get it off of her, but she cannot wriggle it off, it is sticky. And barbed. It is there for the duration. The duration—of what? The duration of something to happen.

The jailer, down on earth walking westward, sees her with his mind. How can she endure it? Why would she choose to feel this pain? She, more than anyone else, has always been kind to him. She was kind even when he was mean. She gave him the beautiful leather suit, asked him to tea when no one else had in 30 years.

∿

Glenn has made his way to the tourist district, where the boys have swimmers' builds and the food is the best in the city. Along the way he's had a bath in the house of an amiable old lady he snookered, bought five great outfits with her credit cards, and is now sitting in the verdant outdoor café of the city's leading Viennese coffeehouse, drinking impossibly strong coffee out of a cup with a charming blue-flowered pattern.

From the next table, two men look over at him curiously. "I think we've met before," says the good-looking middle-aged one with sharp creases in his oddly elegant gray pants and shirt. He elbows the other guy: "Rathbaum, doesn't this fellow look familiar?"

"Oh yeah, sir, a lost family friend." They smile at each other and then Glenn.

"You look like an old buddy of ours."

Glenn nods in his patrician way. He accepts their interest as his due, and then nods to accept a piece of their almond croissant. Glenn asks Gray for a light because he wants to smoke the pack of Gauloises he picked up at Donnaville's excellent tobacconist. As a child, Donna had visions of herself as an impossibly rich man in a velvet smoking jacket enjoying cigars, so the tobacconist's shop in her brain is replete with everything.

∾

Nehemiah and the harlequin are fucking. OH MY GOD the harlequin has never felt so open as Nehemiah's delicious candy dick goes into and then out of him, oh my God there are no obstacles, not one, it is just sliding, what he feels is just honey and delicious fucking, in, in, in and out, he can feel his body sucking on Nehemiah's delicious sausage and chewing on it, yes, yes, yes, he is chewing on it, it is mine, I will get what I need, forever.

∾

Donna at the age of the smoking jacket fantasy—eight, as it happens—wanted to be a mafioso. She had learned the term from reading *Honor Thy Father*, a book about the Bonanno crime family. To Donna, it meant she would be the most powerful man in New York City, so extraordinarily rich she could wear fancy silk suits and sip scotch whenever she wanted to. She could get anything she wanted (she believed), from anyone, man or woman. She could get women to do whatever she wanted.

∽

Thankfully, Glenn has never filled in for me as husband to E. At times, though, he has definitely (even eagerly) filled in for me as a left-wing journalist. Letting my personal hurts guide me as though they were the same as political principles. Loving the powerful or the good-looking or those who were nice to me, and taking that (at times) as though it were the same thing as loving justice, loving kindness, and loving truth.

∽

Falhófnir breathes softly, thinking of his lady friend Greta and her cunt like a thatch of velvet he could not believe he was allowed to put his penis in.

—Hylas wakes abruptly where he'd fallen asleep in the sand. There is a dry dull taste in his mouth. "I need water."

Falhófnir goes down on two knees so the boy can mount. Then the horse takes them swiftly from the desert, not stopping until he gets to a certain convenience store near the eastern boundary of Donnaville.

"Bob's Corner Store," the young man reads aloud. Just behind the little shop is something that shocks him—a great black wall made of a substance he cannot identify, with no apparent gaps, extending as far as he can see in both directions. The wall seems infinitely high, because whenever Hylas tries to look at something over it, the wall gets higher.

"What's up? Y'all really don't want me to leave Donnaville, do you?"

Still, he treads heavily into the store.

"Please, I have no money, but I really need a drink of water, can I get a cup?"

The proprietor, a sour-looking man in his 60s in a button-down short-sleeved white shirt, surprisingly brings him a whole pitcher with a plastic cup. Hylas stands at the counter and drinks the whole thing down.

∼

The little girl has spent the entire day in the neighborhood of Joe's Laundry, much longer than she meant to. Before curiosity drew her into the cafeteria, she'd expected to leave as soon as she had found some food. But after dinner (a second meal!), with night falling, the child peers at the old people sitting around the table and wonders how to say goodbye before she has to slink off to find a place to sleep. Magreet is losing at pinochle and griping about it, but she stops abruptly and gives the child a soft look.

"Child, you'll want a proper sleep before you tackle the bramble tomorrow, and I have the best guest bed."

The old woman's habitation is a good deal away from anything else in the neighborhood, and the child can see the house long before they approach, a large twisty-looking gray-black edifice on a peninsula abutting a shimmery lake. (Wow, a lake. It is the only lake in Donnaville.) The house is made up of triangles and rhombuses sitting atop one another or overlapping, like a black and gray wizard's hat with a few dents in it.

"Why is your house all the way over there?"

"I like to be alone. It is a marvelous and unequaled pleasure!"

"Then why did you invite *me*?"

Magreet cackles. "Don't worry, I don't like the taste of little girl! I invited you because you need a good night's sleep!"

The child is thoughtful as they make the long trek around the lake. She is looking at the sparkly water, wondering how it can be radiant and dark at the same time.

"The water likes you," Magreet says.

"How—how come it likes me?"

∾

The vampires in the jail have begun eating each other. Two have seized on the third and are sucking the marrow out of his legs, then, as they hold him by the neck from the front and behind, opening his chest cavity and sucking out his heart. They find him tasty and sexy. Even if not as ripe and nutritious as somebody who is not a vampire.

Glutted for now, the other two rest on the banker's desk and the check writing stand, hoarsely giggling because the furniture still smells of Khachiya and Sloppy.

∾

Kleine is having a bath in Anna and Frank's bathroom, which is sparkly pink and gold and very clean. There is a little altar in the corner with a figure of a pudgy, euphoric, naked goddess cracking up laughing. A medallion at the bottom says her name: Baubo. She is adorned with rose petals.

Last night was the best thing that's happened to her in a long time, but what comes to her mind as she lies in the bathwater is how she misses the harlequin. She thinks she and he could be close—so close. Why does he keep trying to make her feel small? He is so big already, he seems capable of escaping the bounds of space and time. Why would he need to get even bigger?

He loves to be less close to her, while still being completely connected. The further apart he gets while being joined to her, the happier he becomes. Like one side of an accordion when the other side is as far away from it as possible.

CHAPTER 10

"It's hard to put in words why the water likes you, but the easiest way to say it would be that the water likes you because you are a unique sort of person. And also, well, because you have heart."

"What does that mean, to have heart?"

They are entering Magreet's gigantic house now. Inside, the walls are sparkly black, as though the lake had come inside, and there are roses growing on vines on the living room wall.

"It means you care about things, and people. And about yourself."

"I was told it was very bad and selfish to care about myself."

"You were told a lot of cockamamie things." Magreet honks her nose loudly on a fuchsia-flowered handkerchief. "I'll go check if the feather coverlet for your bed is clean."

∼

Nehemiah and Bobby wake curled around each other in the sprawling nightly rental room above the bar. It is strangely cavernous and dark, but they make a tight meaty ball together in one corner.

This is so much better than the prison, Nehemiah thinks. The people who suggested he get out were right. Nehemiah extends an enormous, gentle forefinger and tickles Bobby's chest and belly, simply because he likes him.

∽

The jailer has arrived at the outside of the Key Food. This neighborhood is more sparsely populated than the rest of Donnaville, but also scarier. Something hits his calf, embedding itself painfully where his pants meet his skin. Teenage boys laugh. He sprints inside before the next bottle hits the spot where he was standing, aiming for his head.

∽

Magna remains on the hook.

∽

Anna sits at the kitchen table, waiting for Kleine to emerge from the bathroom. Kleine is a marvel, she is "brilliant" as the British say, but it is the mother Anna misses now, deep in her belly, in her stomach, in her lungs, the soft hollow in her chest, in her empty hands and feet. She wants to hold Magna and put her hands and feet around her like a monkey might. She wants to climb holding her, as one holds a baby while climbing a tree.

∽

In the artsy tent encampment, Spliffy and Hans now have regular chores to do on the chore wheel and dishes they prepare when it's their night in the kitchen. They can't quite believe it themselves. "You're becoming a bit bourgie, sis," Hans says with a twinkle in his eye as they make spaghetti for 100.

In fact, Spliffy is the one who's always been terrified of becoming bourgie. "Look at us!" Hans has had to say to her numerous times on the street, pointing to the dirt on their clothes and the plastic water bottles they took from the trash to reuse as cups. "Do you really think we're in danger of becoming billionaires?"

Now Spliffy turns and snickers. "I never had my hands on such nice ingredients for making sauce before, that's for sure!" There are large dented cans of whole tomatoes, a bushel of onions, and some garlic that fell off the back of a truck.

After dinner, there will be a weekly public performance night, and Spliffy will combine improvised poetry with a dance involving scarves. She's always wanted to dance. In her hands one red scarf and one black one will entwine like snakes. They will even be seen to rise into the sky, hissing, in the direction of the prison, like the magician Aaron's snakes before the Pharaoh.

~

The child's guest room in Magreet's house is on its own special landing, high up near the top of the house. A triangular room, like many in this lodging. There is a large open window across from the bed, and through it the child can see the full moon.

"The air up here is very nice, especially on a night like this," the bony old lady smiles at her. Her jagged teeth are still at 45 degrees to one another, but somehow the smile seems friendly. Magreet is wearing fuzzy cotton pajamas with hippos on them.

"How is the temperature for you? Would you like it to stay open?"

The child nods yes. The air smells like piñon and something sweet and midnight-ish. It is cold, but she likes it. She lies on the feathery bed, and the old lady puts the coverlet on her. She has brought a silvery pitcher full of water and another curious silvery object. "If you need me for anything, ring this bell."

∽

Inside the supermarket, the jailer curiously peruses the fruit section, full of so many colorful, glimmering things he has never eaten before. He remembers how one lady his mother visited would give him a pomegranate for Rosh Hashanah, and he cannot forget the little jewels of the seeds and their tart wild juiciness. He would smell one of the fruits laid bare before him, ripped open like something bloody, but sparkly, beautiful, then burst a seed hard in his mouth, he remembers nothing more sensual from his childhood.

Always, he wished his mother's friends knew what she did to him.

After, they would take him to live in their homes. They would stop adoring his mother. She would be disgraced and reduced to—

An odd sensation at his ankles makes the jailer look down. A rat has been brushing its whiskers lightly against the jailer's bare feet.

"What is it you want there, little boy?" Something about the rat makes the jailer unusually gentle.

Something about the little rat brother also makes him feel more serene and sure, as though he himself had a right to exist.

The rat points with his head, indicating that the jailer

should follow. Moving purposefully, at a great clip, the little fellow brings the jailer all the way to the other side of the store, past the frozen TV dinners, the detergents, endless aisles of canned tomatoes and soda, all the way to the meat section.

Underneath a great pile of murdered pork shanks, something is calling to the jailer: "Open me!"

He is nonplussed. He reaches under the pork shanks to find a standard white business envelope bursting with ambiguous contents. When he pulls off the tape holding the swollen thing closed, inside is a rock somehow married to a piece of industrial metal. It looks like a little boomerang, or a dark jagged ball with wings. With it is a tiny, dirty page ripped from a memo pad, in the unmistakable handwriting of his mother: "I am real sorry, David."

∼

At Bob's Corner Store, Hylas has chugged the entire pitcher of water. After lying back down on the wood floor for three breath cycles, he stands up ramrod straight and goes outside to talk to Falhófnir.

"I need to see the harlequin, please take me!" Falhófnir gives him his warmest look yet and indicates he should mount. Together they shoot across the territory of Donnaville till they arrive at the gay bar where Nehemiah and Bobby are holding each other in the upstairs room.

∼

The child looks out at the moon. Its light grows warmer and more beckoning. The moon comes through the window and charms her, so she finds herself relaxing, something completely unusual for her. She feels warm from the moon's light despite the cold pouring through the window, and she smells something intoxicating, quickening her blood.

From the inky black air outside, a hazy, insubstantial thing pours into the room, a dull cloud with a little light behind it, gradually taking shape next to the window. A beautiful woman, majestic. Long hair of an indistinct whitish color. She stands there hovering in midair, looking straight at the child. A long, lacy white dress hugs her comely body. The woman's eyes don't have any irises in them, like Little Orphan Annie's.

She says: "I am the bad mother."

The child screams.

∼

Falhófnir stays outside while Hylas goes into the bar.

"I'm looking for a very beautiful man, about yea tall—"

"Aren't we all, honey!" says the bartender listlessly.

"No, I heard that he's here, he has long golden hair to here," Hylas indicates his shoulders, "Very butch and femme at once—"

"Well, he's upstairs honey, but you don't want to see him right now." The bartender points his thumb toward the ceiling.

"Why not?"

"Well, he's got company, baby."

Hylas stands very still for a moment and breathes. He thinks.

"I can take company."

"Knock first."

Hylas goes up the steps, feeling the solid wood beneath his feet. The door at the top of the stairs is made of highly polished ebony, dark and bright. He knocks loudly.

"Who's there?" Bobby's melodious voice rings out, powerful as always.

"It's Hylas."

The door flies open. The harlequin sails up to him and clasps him hard.

"Oh, thank God, " says the harlequin. "Fuck, I was so worried about you." The squeeze he gives Hylas around the shoulders is warm. Then he rubs the young man's skinny body, caressing his arms and neck and head gently. As the warmth of these caresses envelops him, Hylas feels more cared for than he has ever been in his adult life.

Suddenly Bobby pulls back and looks at his face curiously: "Hey, you look a little different."

Hylas takes that in for a painful second. "It's still me." He clasps Bobby back, just as hard, ignoring the fact that Bobby is naked and the other man in the room, a huge, crazily muscular giant sitting on the bed, is naked, too.

∼

Kleine comes out of her bath and diffidently goes up to where Frank and Anna are sitting at the kitchen table, eating pancakes now formed in the shape of vulvas, breasts, and female hands. She would skulk out of the apartment unobserved if she could, but it's too late. She wishes she'd decamped before she took her bath. Her usual M.O.: get up early in the morning before the other party is awake, get sneakers on before the other party is fully conscious, move out quickly on the dawning streets until she gets so far away that the sun is high in the sky.

"Have some labia!" Frank says, handing her a plate.

"There's coffee," Anna tells her sweetly, soft hand on her arm.

Well fuck it. This is nice. I'm going to eat some pancakes.

The sweet cardamom syrup Anna and Frank have for pancakes, from a small syrup-maker somewhere in Donnaville's mountains, wakes her up. And the coffee's good.

∼

The child rings the bell.

The apparition comes closer, arms curving forward trying to embrace her, the whole thing floating over to where the child lies near the headboard. The little girl stands up on the bed and grabs a pillow. Her leather arm protectors are radiant on her forearms.

"You forgot about me, didn't you?" the beautiful hazy woman says. Her eyes still have no irises, and her feet are hovering six inches above the coverlet, a mere foot away from the child. "You forgot about me, but did you really think I would leave you alone?"

"Get out!" Magreet shouts, sprinting through the door and attacking the ghostly visitor with a huge wooden stick. "Get the fuck out of here!" And she hits the hazy woman on the head so hard that despite the latter's insubstantiality, the child can hear something go CRACK!

The bad mother screams. "You hurt me! I feel very hurt!"

Magreet smacks her again, across the eyes. The bad-mother-in-outline yelps, and jumps out the window.

"I'm sorry she came in here." Magreet is not the huggy sort, but she jumps on the bed and grasps the child around the shoulders, at a mere six inches' distance. For her, this is a warm embrace. "I didn't think she would dare to come into my house. I thought the benefit of the beautiful night outweighed the risk."

The child remembers the stars outside, the excitement of the air. It was crisp as a fall apple.

"I daresay it did you good."

The child is amazed. "You knew she might come?"

"Everything that lies dormant about an individual comes in my window when they sleep in that room, if the window's open to the full moon. It is very helpful and lucky!"

∼

Glenn returns with Officers Rathbaum and Gray to their outsize, swank apartment a few streets over from the Viennese coffeehouse. A lot of guys are there, shirtless or in uniform tank tops from various armies of occupation that are not the official security force of Donnaville: the IDF, the US Marines, the CBP. They are dancing, and a cheery whiff of pot smoke hovers over the crowd.

"These boys keep our city safe, Glenn," Lieutenant Gray, one arm on Glenn's shoulder, points to the dancing men. "Don't you forget it."

"They look very brave," Glenn avers. "How are they coping with the emptying of the prison?"

"Prisoner levels rise and fall, Glenn, rise and fall, throughout the history of Donnaville. We hold the power here regardless, while the prison stands."

Glenn remembers the jailer applying the nutcracker to his testicles. None of Gray's security officers ever tortured him, as far as he can recollect. He does have a faint memory of Rathbaum, Pepowitz, Smith, and Gray bringing him into the prison in the first place, crashing him down on the floor like an unwieldy package, and hitting him with truncheons in his kidneys, groin, knees, and across the nose. Did it happen more than once?

Whoof. He breathes the memory away. It was a long time ago. The jailer is the one he really hates. These men seem to be his friends.

"You make sure that everything goes okay."

"We make sure that everything goes okay." Gray's iron face has a satisfied look.

"You keep the order here."

"We keep things running smoothly. Know that if we ever leave this place, Donna will fucking fall apart."

"I should be rooting for you to leave, then," Glenn laughs.

It takes a minute for Gray to get the joke. Then he guffaws uncontrollably. "Aha-ha-ha-ha-ha-ha!"

∼

The divine mother has learned to breathe in rhythm with her agony. A wave of pain will start from the top of her skull, build as it descends her throat, and crest as it raids the middle of her guts. Then rushes out her *dan tien*, the most holy place in her body, with a sense of her vital force exiting. Another way to say this: First she feels the sensation of stabbing, then the sensation of being cut. Then gagging as the esophagus "swallows" the hook, then the utter torment, eventually burning off at her *dan tien*. So it goes: Stab cut hurt gag-and-swallow burn. Stab cut hurt gag-and-swallow burn. She breathes along with it, as though she were birthing a baby.

What does it mean that the hook comes out of her at her *dan tien*, which is called "the golden stove"?

∼

When E is very sad, Donna sometimes gets terrified. What will happen if E goes inside forever with her sadness, and all Donna will be able to see for her remaining time on earth is E's face, closed? Not looking at her, not able to connect. She imagines not being able to bear it. E's face next to her but no one home. No one's eyes there, passionate as E's eyes usually are, seeing and engaging in an almost erotic manner with her own. E not looking at her, not talking to her ever. Donna stranded, deserted alone with her feelings forever.

∼

In her village defined by storage units, Mala sees more people falling sick by the day. She is no longer charging anyone to stay there, and she spends her time nursing people for 10 hours out of every 24. Standing on the outside of her encampment, she raises her arms to a cloudy sky and calls in a screeching whisper *Falhófnir*!

And the horse is there, whinnying at her.

"I need help. People are getting sick. We need to do something."

Falhófnir looks at her steadily. She gets on his back and he takes her, riding not flying, clear south to the prison.

∼

A sweet yellow light enters in the child's huge window, and she wakes to the scent of coffee and healthy, almond-butter sugar buns.

"Wow, coffee!" the child says. "I haven't had that since the old days, when my mother used to put—" She pauses, beet red. She turns her face down.

Magreet puts her hand gingerly on the child's tricep. Suddenly, she is pulling the child close and hugging and squeezing her without, this time, the six-inch invisible barrier between them.

The child says "Mmpfh!", surprised as air is forced out of her. "Hey! I've got to go. I have to make it to the bramble today."

"You need to drink that coffee first," Magreet says. "And eat all those buns, I made them for you!"

∼

The jailer is sitting outside the Key Food, leaning up against its back wall and weeping. The rat is with him, comforting him by swooshing its tail gently against his legs.

"David is my name," he tells the rat. "She hardly ever called me that. I forgot what I was supposed to be called."

In its teeth, the rat carries the strange half-rounded, half-jagged sculptural thing made of curved metal and stone, the thing that had come in the envelope along with the note from the jailer's mother—from David's mother. The rat deposits the thing at David's feet.

"What the fuck is that, anyway?" David asks. It is about as big as a tiny cave dwelling bat.

∼

"Hey there, dude!" says Nehemiah, waving from the bed at Hylas, who is still embracing the harlequin by the door. "I'm Nehemiah, buddy, why don't you come right over here and say hello!"

Hylas sits down on the bed, feeling unusually open, and takes him in. He likes Nehemiah—this man is big, happy, powerful, friendly, and sexy. He shakes the man's hand gently. "Hi, sweetie. I'm Hylas."

Over by the door the harlequin smiles, and his smile looks lavish, quite real. "Why don't we all grab some breakfast?"

∼

"I have to go to work," says Anna, running a finger lightly along Kleine's midsection.

"Sigh," says Kleine.

"Aw, you'll see each other again," laughs Frank. They are still around the table, with little chewed remnants of breast and labia and lip pancakes on their plates. They have already scarfed down all the pancakes depicting women's hands. "Anyhow, don't you have to go to work too, Kleine? What do you do for work, anyway?"

"I don't really have a job," Kleine says with embarrassment. "I just get by here and there. With, ah, this and that."

"Aw, no worries, honey. People don't have to have a regular job to be real or important. Capitalism sucks, and don't I know it!"

"What do you do for work, Frankie?"

"Work in midtown," he makes a face. "A receptionist."

∼

Magreet had said goodbye to the child at the twisty house, packing her up some egg sandwiches, water, and a thermos of hot tea for the journey to the bramble, where there is not even one convenience store. In a little rucksack, which Magreet had slung over the child's shoulder, the bony old lady had also carefully folded underwear, long sleeved T-shirts, socks, and a pair of long pants made of a curious material.

Then she'd kissed the girl on the top of her forehead and bid her march along the lake. "It'll get your blood flowing! Goodbye, my dear."

But here is Magreet again as the child comes finally, sweating, red-faced, to the end of the lake. The child has marched around in a circle. But if it's possible for anyone to stand vehemently, emphatically, steadfastly, Magreet is standing vehemently and firmly on the dusty road to the west along with Cantaloupe, Espardenya, Jasper, and tall Alyia, who looms over all the old people like the great black water bird known as the anhinga. Cantaloupe, gorgeous in a Creamsicle-colored silk blouse that the child notices shows most of her bosoms, reaches out a veiny, beringed hand smelling of jasmine and gently pats the child's light brown hair.

"Goodbye, cutie!" she says. "I can't wait till you come back and see us again, even if it's a lot of years from now." Cantaloupe's hand is surprisingly strong, but it doesn't hurt. The child takes in the smell of jasmine, keeps it.

Jasper hands the child a piece of black chocolate fruit cake. "It's for now," he says, "for nibbling as you walk."

Espardenya bends down to her and says, "I am giving you this little poem:
Make much of your speeches
But don't accept leeches
Oh you deserve peaches
And far ocean reaches."

The child feels confused, but kisses Espardenya on his shaggy head as he crouches.

Alyia grabs the child, picks her up and holds her aloft at the level of Alyia's own head: "This is your kingdom." And she shows her not just the mountains where the harlequin dwells three days' march away near Donnaville's southern border, but distant mountains in every direction, the shapes of shining distant mountains past the bramble, past the river's farthest shore, everywhere. "Never forget. *All* of it is your kingdom."

Then she sets the child gently down on the soft black earth. The girl abruptly kisses her, then runs up to each of the old people in turn and give them a big wet kiss where their lips meet their cheek. Magreet is last, and the child hangs on the bony old lady's neck for a long time. Then she sets her feet down purposefully on the road to the bramble. Before the child takes the final step, Alyia dashes forward, crouches and touches the child's luminous leather arm protectors. With a rueful smile: "Don't forget these. They are needful."

∼

Kleine is walking up to midtown from Frank and Anna's digs looking for more coffee, a sandwich. (Egg, cheese, and bacon maybe? Sex always makes her hungry.) A black horse suddenly shoots down from the sky, right onto the dirty street.

"Falhófnir! Cutie!" She winds her arms around his neck and squeezes. The horse looks at her with his troubled, dark intelligent eyes.

"Something wrong? I thought so. We did that jailbreak thing all half-assed, amirite?"

The gelding snorts. Thoughtfully, she gets on his back. Falhófnir speeds down the sidewalk, scared passersby falling out of the way left and right, till they're in front of the bank. Stretched out in a leisurely manner at the top of the stairs is a woman in a red bandanna. Jibing in some way with her long, scraggly-curly blond hair and acne scars, her many tattoos depict scenes of mayhem—murder, knifings, rape. Kleine steps back, gasping.

"Those things are written on my skin so that they don't have to happen," tough Mala says, sitting up and looking straight at her. "Hello."

∼

Now that David has his name, he wants to dress differently, he finds. He really would like to take a shower and discover how he would like to groom himself. What should he do with his hair? What kind of vibe does he want to give off?

He takes the strange object his mother left for him to a crumbling picnic table under a tree abutting the Key Food. The little rat goes with him. This is a good place to think. He will need to contemplate where he can take a shower, how to get new clothes, how to do everything differently.

From far off, he feels Magna's body sliding slightly around on the hook that burns her all over. It hurts now even in her legs and feet, even though the hook emerges from her body a good ways above them. It hurts her now to be alive, simply that. As he now participates in all her feelings, he perceives this, too: she actually wishes she were dead. How can he think about clothing and hair at a time like this?

∼

In the divine mother's fortress, her attendants go about their business. The llamas have decided to mate because it is not likely she will need them anytime soon. They mate with each other first, then gamely with a bunch of llamas of various sexes from a nearby fortress. The worms write messages to their mother in the soil, writing with their bodies. They aver that they will always love her, tell her to take hope because change, at least, comes for everyone in the end. Magna's raven Introspection is inconsolable and will not leave the little house she made for it out of white canvas in the living room. Her doodies, jumping out of the composting toilet, fret and tell stories about her acts of great bravery and kindness as they sit around a bonfire the way Magna herself used to sit around it with her guests.

Lieutenant Gray, who has now rechristened himself Captain Gray of the Sacred Donnaville Guard, has bought new uniforms for everyone, so much nicer than the dingy gray-green ones they used to wear. These are bright black and sexy, with leather caps for everybody and ceremonial white braided cords, called aiguillettes, attached like miniature lassos to the left shoulder. They have shiny black boots with eagle emblems on the back.

"Everybody keep those uniforms SPICK-AND-SPAN!" Gray booms to the boys, about 30 of them, as they all attempt to meet covertly in the Viennese coffeehouse garden. Everyone is clutching a strong, well-made espresso drink, because Gray doesn't stint when it comes to payment or good catering. People need A REASON to save Donnaville, and after his experience with the jailer, Captain Gray no longer trusts those who are motivated by selflessness or principle. Glenn, looking good in a turtleneck and blazer, sits with the boys: he will be the journalist to document this effort. Gray had slipped him a uniform as well, but Glenn feels a need to uphold the standards of his profession. (He will only wear the uniform in private.)

∾

Scraps of sausages, potatoes, and tiny bits of fried egg remain on the table, but hardly anything is left. The harlequin, Nehemiah, and Hylas ate it all. There are empty mugs of beer and giant porcelain cups of coffee in a size once originated by Starbucks.

Nehemiah burps appreciatively, stands, and winks: "Well, I'll leave you to it, then."

After he has gone, Hylas's face changes. It turns darker and a bit redder, yet he reaches out and grabs both of the harlequin's hands in his own. "When I woke up at the inn that day, you weren't there. Why did you leave me, Bobby?"

The harlequin feels a curious storm rising in his chest. He lets the storm out, which he can't remember having done before. "My name's not Bobby."

Hylas swears, very creatively.

"I am very sorry that I lied to you. I . . . I have never told anyone my real name. I do want to be with you, though. Hylas, listen, my name is Zosimos."

∼

Anna would rather be doing so many other things on this languid, pleasant morning than go to work at the kitchen. Specifically, she would like to kiss Kleine's crazily soft eyes tenderly and then fuck her brains out. But here she is at her station, and baking is her life's work, and she loves her handheld apple pies as much as it is possible to love anything inanimate. They're not going to make themselves.

Apples on her station, red, yellow, and green, now, bizarrely, actually begin to whisper to her, a sound like hissing: "Make us. Make us." "Make us."

They've never spoken to her before. She bends her head down to the latticed ceramic fruit bowl, more than a little freaked out. Just then she hears something murmuring to her from the small glass jar of smoked cinnamon. This is getting strange. Then higher-pitched, screamier sounds from the extra-fat butter and the sour cream. What are they all saying? "Make us. Make us! Make us!" Frowning, she turns the oven on. The ingredients have never demanded to be denatured and remade into things before.

"Honey, can you pipe down over there?" Conchetta calls from her station. So she can hear it, too.

"I'm sorry," Anna calls back. "I don't understand what's happening."

Then from the window she hears a weird loud neigh like a yell. She isn't easily distracted while she works, but she coasts to the window, unaware of her feet moving. Right out there is a beautiful, jet-black horse. Even odder, on this queerest of days, the horse is giving her a look whose meaning is impossible to mistake: *Come now. Forget the food.*

The ingredients try furiously to drown the gelding out. "Make us!" the balls of extra-hot nutmeg cry. "Make me!" says one with a pronounced chip on its shoulder, "make me!" Feeling dizzy, Anna grabs her jacket and sprints for the exit. As she flees, a sheet of phyllo dough jumps up off the table in her face, crumples in two, and yells, "Make me, you fucking bitch!"

∼

The road to the bramble is dusty and unseasonably hot. It is also boring: there are only dried-up grasses plus black insects that dart toward the child's face, legs, and neck. She is wearing the long purple silk shirt, and her legs stick out underneath. Crows call from a long way off. There are no distractions in the hazy sunlight, and she is unable to screen out the memory of her mother pouring a little of her own coffee into the child's glass of milk, making it taste delicious, sophisticated.

Her mother.

The child would rather think of the jailer. When she last saw him, he was in the glowing green oval she had caught him in for his safety. The green cloud was supposed to provide a kind of stasis, but would it really have kept him from being torn to pieces by the people he'd harmed?

"Did you really think I would leave you alone?" the bad mother asks her again, in her memory. She's going to keep seeing the image of her mother all along this route, floating six inches above the floor, scaring her. "I haven't forgotten you," repeats the mother from last night's visitation. The child stops in her tracks and takes a quarter of a sandwich out of her pack, puts it in her mouth. Magreet painted the bread with some special kind of hot mustard the child has never had before. *It is so good.* Now she calms her mind, making the walking into a meditation. Foot one, foot two, inhale. Exhale. Look at the sky. Foot one, foot two. Look.

∼

On the hook, in her fortress, Magna sees the child from far off, endlessly walking, a small figure, tramping to the very western edge of Donnaville. She tries to touch the little girl with her mind. Does the child detest her, too? Does the child hate her love? Hope never to feel it again? Never to feel that warm, milky, nurturing feeling seduce her with its kindness?

"*Sweetaleh*," Magna calls down to the child. She is trying to feel all of the pain that is inside her, so she can use her strength to reach the child, instead of keeping Magna safe from her own agony. She had not thought it possible for the pain to get even worse, but it does. Her vision becomes livid purple energy strokes, black lightnings. Gray-black snakelike swirls. She reels, and would collapse were it not for the hook holding her in place. She staggers, while upright. She's not sure how much more of this her living bodymind can take. Even a goddess is fragile, inside a human body. But she calls to the child: "Child! My child! My own one. I love you."

From far off, the child, walking on the dusty road, feels love aimed at her across miles of air . . . across entire weather systems . . . across the vast electrical currents powering Donnaville's synapses . . . it hits her right upside the head, and she lurches for a moment. "Mommy?"

∼

"Zosimos . . . are you supposed to be some kind of god? Mala called you 'the king of hell' or something."

"No, that's really more of an old joke. Well, I *was* a god, but I'm not one anymore, not since I met you anyway." Why is he smiling?

"You're *happy* not to be a god?"

Zosimos, formerly known as Bobby, looks unusually calm. His expression is clear, blue eyes looking right at Hylas. "I don't need to be a god. I just need some good friends in my life, some very close connections."

"But why didn't you tell me your right name?"

"I was frightened. I lived in a tiny nut for 50 years. I didn't want anybody to find me, much less talk with me."

"But you had fun. You had sex with all those people."

"Yes," and Zosimos's eyes dart mischievously, "I like fun. Still do."

CHAPTER 11

"What are we doing here, and who, uh,"—and here Kleine, recalling herself, suddenly makes her tone more civil—"who are you?"

Mala answers in a deathly tone, her face pale and her lips distended in an odd approximation of a smile. "Something really bad will happen unless we destroy the prison."

Then she sticks out her hand, and actually smiles. "Hi, I'm Mala."

"You're one of a kind, aren't you?" Kleine thinks the other is very cute, all those upsetting tattoos, prior rictus expression and all. "I'm Kleine."

"So Falhófnir brought you here, did he?"

"Uh, I didn't get here by flapping my arms."

"So how come I haven't—" now Mala finally stands up. "How come I haven't seen you around before?" As she inspects Kleine more intently, her look becomes more provocative.

Kleine blushes. "Dunno. I'm shy and people don't remember me. But we helped free the child from here earlier, the harlequin and I."

"That boy! I love him like a brother, but fuck is he a piece of work."

Kleine feels a rush of sympathy. She's also jealous, though. When did Bobby find time to make friends with this girl? She's not sure if she'll ever see him again. After their fight, they didn't even have a legitimate goodbye, just both sullenly stalked off.

She feels grumpy and tight. Squashed. But unexpectedly her lips move and she says, "I love him, too. What an asshole."

From far off, she sees a long line of men in black approaching from the north of Donnaville, apparently from the gentrified neighborhood near the harbor. "What the fuck is that?"

Mala telescopes her hands into the distance. "Ooh. I don't like what this looks like."

"What? A troop of cosplaying Nazis?"

At that very moment, Falhófnir comes barreling up from the south, Anna atop him.

Anna jumps off. "Babe! Did the Lady send you a message to meet me here?"

"I haven't heard from the Lady in days," says Kleine. "But you, little pie, wow, it's beyond delicious to see you again."

∽

David and the rat, whose name is Hornblower, sit on the side of the road brainstorming where to get him new clothes and a dramatic new hairdo. The rat draws pictures in the sand with its forepaws, sketching out various hairstyles and outfits. Finally in agreement, they rise as one and walk forward into the neighborhood of Joe's Laundry, where in the fog they can barely make out a sign that says Rapunzel, Rapunzel. Hornblower pulls at David's pants leg with his teeth, nudging him in the direction of the storefront, which has a large painting of someone's long golden hair hanging in front.

Inside is a plump, sexy older woman in a gauzy peach caftan. "Wow!" she says when David and Hornblower enter.

"I've never been so honored. Which one of you is the haircut for?"

David laughs. "Me. We were also hoping you could recommend a place nearby where I could get some nice new duds. I'm kind of, um, I'm going through a makeover right now." And he laughs again.

∽

The child has entered on the bramble itself. There is no path. There is a crisscross of canes, no leaves or berries visible. She gasps for a moment, because she cannot even distinguish individual shrubs in that razor-sharp, monstrously large enchainment of stems. Each prickly piece seems connected to the others, as though it were all just one entity, just one hideously impenetrable life-form. She wishes she had thought to ask the old people for a knife, but she turns her new rucksack upside down and there is no knife in there, just food, water, clothes.

Abruptly, she remembers the black fruitcake. It is still in her hand, she has been holding it all this while. Walking back a few paces, so she is out of the bramble and back in the friendly dirt of the road, she sits on the ground and starts eating it. She finds the cake surprising. Both spicy and buttery, tasting of bitter coffee and lavish, heart-thrilling chocolate, it also tastes *nourishing* in a way she never expected from cake. The walnuts and prunes have the highest nutritional value, she estimates, but it is the eggs, butter, and lemon in the cake that make her feel cared for, make her glow.

When the fruitcake is gone, she continues sitting in the dirt, and she examines what she has, spreading the contents of the rucksack out in front of her. She selects a long sleeved shirt and the long pants and changes into them, and having no shoes, improvises by putting socks on her bare feet and covering them with underwear. Then she puts a few more pairs of underwear on her face and ties them to her head with socks.

∽

Hylas and Zosimos are holding temporary hands tenderly in a citylike miniature eternity[1] when their waiter strides over with more force and emphasis than seems strictly necessary. He announces, "There's a horse outside sticking his nose in the door and threatening to ride into the place. I couldn't think of anyone else he might be here for but you two."

"That horse is really kind of annoying, isn't he?" Hylas fusses.

"Something bad must be going down. We have to go."

"Bad like having to end our afternoon together early?"

"Bad like kidnapping and murder." Zosimos pulls him up. "Come on, this way." At the door, the gelding gives Zosimos a long, fond look, the kind you might give a grandchild on his graduation. Both men get on his back.

∽

Glenn is trying to keep up with the boys in uniform as they march on the prison. But he is surprised to discover that his strength was entirely eroded in that place. He can barely lift his feet, trying to keep up with these well-fed gorillas. He tags

---

1. From Allen Ginsberg's poem, "At Apollinaire's Grave," published in *Kaddish and Other Poems*, City Lights Books, 1961.

along at the back of the group as they proudly march down Minkowitz Avenue, the grand boulevard that goes diagonally through the heart of Donnaville. The boulevard has its start near Prospect Park in the gentrified section and carves right through the prison, "the royal road" as the oldest denizens of Donnaville call it. It ends in the southeast of Donnaville, past the art museums and factories and hard by Donna's storehouses and greenhouses. Very early that morning, white vans had taken the troops secretly from the coffeehouse to the monumental plaza where the boulevard begins. From that august setting, with dark-green bronze men on horseback leaping and holding spears above them, they can now, in a march choreographed by a part of Donna that loves the double lightning bolt and the whip, make a grand entrance.

∼

The little girl has added a thick T-shirt tied sharply over each hand. Once inside the bramble, she squirms this way and that, trying out different ways to go forward. The vines give resistance, but like water, their resistance is not absolute. So she squirms a part of her tiny body here and a part there, going deeper, at least she *thinks* it is deeper. It is as though she were swimming through a kind of heavy gelatin threaded through with a thin metallic spiderweb. The bramble is odd, but she maneuvers herself forward slowly, one limb after another, her body moving in a way that's circular but does the job. Surprisingly, nothing here hurts her except when she backs out of a hole that is too small for her and her hair gets caught and pulls.

∼

When Falhófnir arrives at the prison, he gallops all the way up the steps without bothering to let Zosimos and Hylas down. As Mala, Kleine, and Anna scream incomprehensibly to them from below, waving their arms, Falhófnir lifts his massive forefoot and staves in the front door.

"What'd he do that for?" asks Hylas.

"We have to tear this place down," the harlequin explains.

"Why'd you want to destroy it? It looks like a beautiful building."

Before he can answer, Anna, Mala, and Kleine come running up the steps.

"Yep, it's time," Kleine says, as they all hustle inside.

"Babe, do you know what you're doing?" Hylas can't understand why they are vandalizing a bank. Or why Mala from the homeless encampment is here.

But that practical woman, a ring of keys at her belt, snorts, "They're coming!" and motions them all toward the back of the bank lobby, where Zosimos makes a diagonal, sweeping gesture with his arm and suddenly the sideways door appears, its outline all lit up as if by fire. They rush through and they're in the dirty gray prison.

Mala sniffs the air. "No vampire sweat, at least."

Kleine makes a face. "What a pity. What I'm planning would do nicely for them, too." Around her neck, she grimly strokes a tiny iron box that she has hanging on a thin, bright chain.

∾

Cantaloupe spins David around in her barber's chair. "Now, the other way!" she screams.

"Shit! This is fun!"

"I could tell you're on a mission to have more fun in your life! So I wanted to give you some RIGHT NOW!"

This is so nice that David gets out of the chair and bows. On the floor, Hornblower executes a perfect bow to the hairstylist as well.

"So, what do you want to do to your hair?"

"Well, I'm not even sure this is possible, but—" David grimaces and screws up his face, hoping against hope. "Can you make my hair longer? It's too short now."

Cantaloupe scrutinizes his wavy, oily, black-with-a-little-gray locks, cut in a 1950s businessman's DA like Ronald Reagan.

"I can do that. You're gonna need to do a lot of dirty dancing, though."

"What?"

"Dirty dancing. That is the process. Meet here in 10 minutes and dance for the seniors, and your hair will grow."

∽

David just has time to run his body under the shower in the back of the salon. He puts on a homey, fuzzy bathrobe hanging on a beautiful oaken hook. Then he and the little rat brother look around curiously for the clothing he's supposed to wear for the dance.

Hornblower leads the way through a warren of hidey-holes behind the bathroom, searching and searching. While there is a lot of interesting apparatus back there that both of them would like to try out, nothing looks remotely like a set of dancing clothes.

Just then Cantaloupe reenters the shop, followed by a brace of old people.

"Where's my outfit?"

"Outfit? Oh—" she laughs, loudly but gently. "No, my traveling friend, there is no outfit. You're to dance naked for us."

Naked?

∽

In the bramble, the child feels something strange. She feels like she is in her element (she has never felt in her element before). The razor-sharp canes now seem no more threatening than a warm bath, protected as she is by her given and her improvised clothing and her talent for maneuvering through. By swimming through the bramble carefully, snaking her body here and there but constantly moving further inside, she's become one with it. She can sense that she is near its center. It is warm here.

On the hook, the mother looks down and smiles, seeing the child in the heart of the bramble. Even in her pain, she almost giggles to see David pondering, mid-decision, hands hesitating longingly at the bow with which he's tied his robe, as Cantaloupe, Jasper, Espardenya, and Magreet watch.

∽

The men goose-step down the avenue. Their uniforms are sparkly black. They kick the concrete with their boots as though they were stamping on a human face.

At the front, Obersturmbannführer Gray leads the troop, pointing and swirling with his bayonet rhythmically.

Before they get to the prison, Gray has some soldiers in the front throw live grenades into the street so that bodies will fall and passersby scatter in terror as they go by. Word spreads quickly, and from the safety of half a block away the people of Donnaville turn out to watch as the Sacred Donnaville Guard kick their legs forward in unison to retake this territory.

~

Kleine is making a fire. First she makes her companions go back into the savings-and-loan lobby and chop up the bankers' desks, chairs, and check-writing tables. It's a crazy-making task, considering that they don't have any hatchets. But Falhófnir's strong legs, not to mention Mala's bashing against the wood continuously with an old fire extinguisher, do the trick. They have Hylas jump up and down on the weakened furniture fragments till they crumple into convenient-sized firelogs. Meanwhile, Anna gathers up several armfuls of surveillance files and criminal records from the prison's dingy office. These will serve as kindling.

They haul everything back into the prison foyer, still scary and sad with puddles of urine, vomit, and the remnant of Khachiya and Sloppy's blood. Kleine takes the miniature tinderbox she had been carrying around her neck and plays with the tiny flint and firesteel inside.

"Glad you thought to bring that," the harlequin tells her quietly, appearing suddenly by her side.

"You provided all the helpful equipment last time. Decided it was my turn."

"Hey, I'm really sorry I was such an asshole when I saw you last. I do that whenever I like somebody a lot, I can't imagine why. But I don't want to hurt you again. You're the best friend I've ever had."

She looks at him, surprised. "You're joining me for a Diet Coke after we're all done here. With lemon slices, popcorn, and pizza."

∼

All four old people, plus David and his rat, stand in a circle. They're all directly in front of the salon's enormous window, so that anyone who passes by can get a good look. Brilliant sunlight streams in, making the stylist's chairs and her equipment sparkle. Hornblower licks David's calves encouragingly, then rubs his whiskers meaningfully along the bottom of David's fuzzy robe.

But the former jailer of Donnaville must stop for a moment to think. David steps out of the circle, slows down. He becomes infinitely slow, as though he were Conchetta's ragu, so thick it can barely move off the spoon. He forces himself to notice everything: Espardenya's black widow's peak, Jasper's rosy cheeks like a thin Santa Claus, the friendly dust in the crannies of the salon. He smells the half of an iced cruller waiting for Cantaloupe on her desk. Magreet, in overalls today, smells like an agreeable mix of patchouli and turpentine. Abruptly, like a scalded cat, David strides into the center of the circle.

"Do any of you have appropriate music for this?"

Espardenya flies out the door. Before you can say *fire and tongs*, he is back with some instruments: an accordion, a clarinet, a bass, and a tuba. After he hands the accordion, tuba, and bass off to the others, the four old people launch into the vigorous polka tune, "Will You Teach Me How to Yodel."

David sticks one hip out.

"Will you teach me how to yodel?" the four elders sing with gusto.

David tears open the tie at his waist.

"My cute little mountain boy!"

∼

"The guards like to hurt people," Zosimos, formerly known as Bobby, is whispering to Hylas. "They feel less nervous when they're marching and everybody is afraid of them. Please help us stop them, or it's going to be bad for everyone in this city."

Hylas gives him a quizzical look.

There is a loud screeching and grating noise from the bank lobby. All six of them look through the sideways portal, and see the broken double doors of the bank shaking. Kleine had tried ineffectually to close them again with a crowbar, a little superglue, and a large credenza from the director's private rooms pushed in front. POUND. Someone is striking the metal hinges and the remains of the reinforced glass. POUND. Then a higher, squealy note. The glass is broken, and they hear booted feet rushing through.

"Get back!" snarls Mala, pushing Hylas and the others away from the sideways door. There, in the prison foyer, they have heaped the timber in an enormous pyre. "Here goes nothin'!" Kleine says, lighting it.

∼

The child has become so comfortable in the bramble that she must have fallen asleep for a moment. Then she feels a little something like the nibble of a fish, a change in the pressure of her new home. The bramble's supportive embrace around her abruptly lessens as a third of it falls away. Something wet, dirty, and sharp flicks at her belly. She kicks out at it.

It is a gaunt but handsome man in a black T-shirt and jeans, who seems to be able to shrink himself to the size of a giant spider when he wants to bite her belly.

"I'm done with you!" the child cries, kicking the vampire in the head. He dives in to bite her jugular as she brings her leather arm protectors up against his mouth. One of them enters him there and she jams its thick pile down his soft wet throat to choke him. Gagging, he crouches into a ball and stabs her with the brutal points of claws on his hands and feet.

~

Glenn doesn't know what to do. He was terrified when people began falling dead in the street as the boys advanced, and a man landed right next to his elbow, half of him blown off by a grenade. He is beginning to think maybe he shouldn't be with the Sacred Donnaville Guard at all, even as a friendly reporter. But "Glennboy!!" Obersturmbannführer Gray shouts at him, delightfully, flinging him by brute force to the front as they batter the ornate doors, which finally shatter with a pleasing abandon. Inside the lobby, Glenn marvels at the 1930s-style mural about labor and capitalism, but Gray picks him up by the shoulders and flings him to the front again as they advance on the back of the lobby to raid, apparently, whatever the fuck is back there.

"Hey, Asshole Glenn! Open that!" Gray gestures to a sideways door, which the journalist can only see by squinting and imagining hard.

"Me! Why do I have to be the one to open it?"

"Because you DO!" And the squad leader throws him through the sideways door face-first. He feels a horrifying searing pain as soon as he hits the other side.

∼

As soon as the flames leap up, Anna sets about figuring out how to keep them all safe. The prison foyer is exceptionally long and narrow, and the flames and the pile of wood underneath them exceptionally tall. First the six of them cling to the walls and try to inch forward sideways, making their bodies as thin as possible. But Falhófnir can hardly flatten himself against a wall, and anyhow he is clamoring to fly off with as many of them as can fit on his back.

"Does this place have a back door?" It is Hylas, sounding none too happy.

"None that I ever heard of," Zosimos starts to say, but the gelding, for his part, neighs, looking in a northwest direction through the walls.

"Enough!" snorts Mala, taking charge. "We're getting out of here."

∼

Glenn is on fire, from his head to his shins. He can smell every hair on his body burning.

"Help me!" he calls to the people around him, several of whom he recognizes as the do-gooders who yearned to free him from prison.

∼

The robe is on the ground now, and David is dancing.

"Did you know that David means beloved?" his mother calls to him from somewhere in the heavens.

He sees himself naked in the hairstylist's mirror, and his body looks different than the last time he looked. Rosy belly below muscular pectorals, round stomach supporting him, his legs not a young man's but strong, even the hairs on his head more alive, and more doughty. From the mirror he can see his nipples glow.

He sticks a leg out from himself, sweeping it as far as it will go. He moves his arms in a similar, swiping diagonal fashion, like the sound of traditional fiddle music, Jewish, Irish, or Kentuckian.

∼

The child hurts, bleeding at the wrists and ankles. An image flashes before her of her daddy, ramming his fist into her face. "Fuck you, Daddy," she whispers, plunging her thick leather arm protector even deeper down the vampire's throat. A beat later, she worries if her father is okay, still protected from attack from within that viscous green cloud.

∼

Mala pushes everyone down on the ground and makes them crawl, low as they can, through the wooden debris, and worm their way underneath the fire to the other side of the prison. Falhófnir alone she allows to fly over the fire, singeing his legs but getting quickly to the end of the debris pile.

Mala pushes Glenn down with the others, and makes him, also, inch beneath the flames.

∾

Obersturmbannführer Gray sees the flames through the sideways door, notices Glenn on fire. He rushes his men back outside onto the street—out the gaping hole in the smashed double doors. "Water!" he cries. "Buckets of water!"

"Obersturmbannführer!" Rathbaum pipes up. "We're just going to let those people go?"

Gray puts his hands around Rathbaum's neck. "Asswipe, if this prison burns down, we're all *dead*, and I mean that literally."

∾

Still dancing, David sidles up to Jasper, who is playing the heck out of the enormous tuba that seems to protrude from his body like an extra limb. "Will you teach me how to yodel?" David sings along with the others, bumping his hip against the lovely old man's, "and fill my heart with joy?"

Magreet, Espardenya, Cantaloupe, and Jasper all give him a warm look. David's nude body is glittering in the light from the windows, and as he dances—Magreet is yodeling boisterously now—his penis slowly becomes erect. They continue looking at him with love.

∼

When they finally get past the flames, Glenn and the prison-breakers find the jailer's cell, long disused. "In here!" Kleine says, and they step, still choking on smoke, past torn-up floorboards, pools of soured milk, buckling and contorted lead. It is the ceremony of spite that Gray and the others have made of the jailer's room. They see the door leading to the rest of Donnaville, the same door the divine mother knocked on less than a fortnight ago, when she asked the jailer of Donnaville if he'd be kind enough to make her a cup of tea. Zosimos pushes it open and out they go.

∼

The child has finally succeeded at twisting off the vampire's head. She rolls away, exhausted, but the bramble is no longer the comfort it was. She crawls away onto the bare soil, still bleeding.

From out of the sky, something rams onto her face. It attaches itself to her and feels sticky, with a pain so sharp it burns. She's shocked at first so that she cannot move, but then she turns her face to the earth and bashes whatever this is against the hard ground of the road.

∼

Zosimos and Hylas, Kleine and Anna, Mala and Falhófnir all run around to the front of the building to make sure the entire prison is burning.

They see a bucket brigade out front, the corn-fed members of the Sacred Donnaville Guard passing each other 50-pound drums of water like they're nothing.

Flames are still rising over the middle of the building, but in the front, all the fires are going out.

"NO!" In her fortress, the divine mother, watching this, is furious. "This is NOT what I want to be happening!" In a sudden burst of strength she shoots her body forward, trying to get the hook off, but the barbs only go in deeper.

David hears her shout, and stops his dance.

"David, you must help them burn it down!" She collapses, arms and legs like a puppet's, still hung from her own ceiling.

Naked, David rises up in the air. He now seems able to fly. Cantaloupe and the others clap for him fiercely, blowing kisses, and the hairstylist opens the door for him. At the last minute, the rat throws something up to David that he's been holding in his teeth: It is the weird crooked amalgam of metal and stone that the erstwhile jailer's mother left for him. David catches it in his hands and flies away.

∼

In the air, he feels something unaccustomed on his shoulders, and he touches his fingers there to find, suddenly, hair: long and black.

Flying, he sees a disturbance over in the west. His heart flutters, because he's not sure what to do. Then he decides and plunges, swiftly, down to where the child keeps trying to pound the last remaining vampire off her face.

He tears at the cruddy, tenacious, searing thing and finally bites it off of her, chewing it to small pieces and stomping on them. But to his disbelief, the little pieces keep trying to fly away, so at last he thrusts them all into his mouth and chews, chews, chews.

"Daddy!"

She puts her arms around his neck and presses her now-shining and strangely long-haired father to her. They have never been so close to occupying the same space, not even when his fist was going in her face. He pulls her up into the wind and, tenderly holding the small of her back, flies with Donna to the center of the city. From the air, looking back at the bramble, she finally sees a rose floating in the center of the canes.

~

Mala and Kleine have their friends gather whatever additional flammables they can from the streets near the prison—advertising sawboards, building scaffolding, wooden pallets. But they're all terrified to get near the members of the Guard, who are still industriously passing drums of water from hand to hand and emptying them with a gush inside the double doors.

One second later, Zosimos and Mala have had enough. Each of them rushes an officer. Mala bashes Guardmember Rathbaum in the head with a two by four. Zosimos knees a strapping young Aryan in the crotch, then stomps on his head once he is down.

That is all it takes for peaceful Anna to dart forward, grind Guardmember Smith's toes under her shoes, and dash his bucket and another guardmember's to the ground. Kleine elbows two officers in the kidneys, so that their drums of water go flying. Even Hylas bites Pepowitz in the face, then punches him in the eye. Finally, Falhófnir acts, dashing forward, hooves in the air, mowing all the other guardsmen down. Kleine, Zosimos, and Mala carry all the wood to the front of the doors, where Kleine, kneeling, sets the improvised kindling on fire.

∽

In the bank lobby—which, admittedly, no longer looks like a bank lobby but a misshapen, fire- and water-damaged place of ash and dirt, Obersturmbannführer Gray is seething. New licks of fire are coming in from outside, even as the fires still smolder in the prison past the sideways door.

He strides out to his officers. And sees, on the steps of the building, his people lying hurt, not a single one upright. He charges straight for Hylas, pinning him face down on one of the low steps, Gray's eagle boot crushing his back.

Zosimos flies right up to Gray and kisses him.

"What?"

While the harlequin pours all of his intoxicating presence into Gray, the others race ahead to the hole in the doors, where they delicately prod and shove the lighted wood inside with sticks and bits of street furniture that have not yet been kindled.

∽

The harlequin is kissing and kissing and kissing Obersturmbannführer Gray as if his life depended on it. The latter, in a daze, stumbles backward, falling away from Hylas. Anna helps Zosimos keep the obersturmbannführer glazed and at peace, guiding the Nazi down to the beginning of the steps and laying him on his back, locked on the harlequin's lips.

Hylas rolls over nearby, groaning. When he sees his boyfriend kissing Gray, he moans.

∼

"How can we make sure the whole thing is on fire without getting burnt to death ourselves?" says Kleine.

They are peering through the great hole in the doors, and she is getting edgy. She drums her fingers along the peeling paint and broken wood.

"We just have to watch it all burn down, until there's nothing left."

How can Mala be so fierce?

"Uh, I don't know what I'm doing here," Hylas says brokenly. He looks into the empty, dirt-filled bank, then back at his boyfriend keeping Gray glued to the ground with his lips.

"Um," says Mala, "you're waiting for your man?"

∼

The goddess speaks in a defeated and sick-sounding voice inside David's head. "I don't know ... if this will do anything ... but you should know ... metal fires ... burn very hot."

David, holding Donna, flies directly over the center of the prison, the very heart of Donnaville. It is glowing red inside there, not from fire but from something else that mysteriously powers the city. But to his eye, the red color keeps flickering back and forth to gray from the filthy barbed wire that stretches, nearly invisible, across its entire length and width. Red, gray, red, gray, red. He finds it sickening. Taunting.

He speaks into the heads of his six companions: "JUMP!"

Glenn, watching the little crew of resisters from the sidelines, thinks he knows how this ends. He runs to the doors, elbowing past Mala and Kleine, thinking to join a remnant of the Sacred Donnaville Guard he believes is in there. There has got to be a whole elite squad still in the prison that will leap out and overwhelm the companions any minute now.

Glenn darts in.

Like a tiny star or a snowflake, the former jailer lets fly the queer, curvy, jagged, metal-and-stone batlike thing his parents gave him, originally, on a very early day over 50 years ago. When his mother left the rough-feeling doodad again for him recently under the pork shanks in the supermarket, it was just a reminder, a keepsake of what he'd already endured in a time almost past memory.

This item falls into the still-standing structure of the prison and explodes.

The resisters, watching, think they might go blind. Green, purple, pink, and orange flames, in flower-shapes so bright they look like the the residue of an atomic bomb, shoot up from the twisty gray hulk that had been the prison. The members of the Sacred Donnaville Guard, including Gray on his back underneath Zosimos, and now including Glenn, all disappear. In the place that had been the prison and the bank, is now an empty field. Grass is growing, small little shoots, and there is no sign of dirt or ash.

Mala looks around, bewildered. She walks a few feet, a disturbed look on her face, shellshocked. "But the jail has always been here."

"I know," says Kleine. "Knowing it was here formed my childhood, and my teenhood, and my adulthood. When I crawled out of my hole, all I wanted to do was something that was *not* being in a jail. That's why I wanted to have sex like 500 times a day. Also, I was furious with Magna and I wanted her to make it up to me."

"I wanted to bake, first because baking is the best thing in the world," Anna says, "but second, because eating hot sweet pies is the very opposite of the prison."

Zosimos shouts "Brother!" And comes to crouch where naked David is sitting with the child in the grass. "You look fantastic! I like the hair."

David hugs his brother, unbothered by his own nakedness. Zosimos kisses him in damp little kisses all over his cheeks.

Then Zosimos twirls the little girl in the air. "How you doing, you little wondergirl? I heard you did so good out there!"

"Papa, I have a name I didn't remember," she tells him, climbing on his shoulder and playing with his ear.

"I have a name I didn't remember, either," David tells the little one and Zosimos. "Both of you, my name is David."

"David!" says the harlequin. "I'd forgotten what your real name was. And I knew my own name, but I never told anyone what it was till today. Both of you, my name is Zosimos."

The child takes both of their hands in her own and crosses them. Then she puts their hands on her own nose, giggling and wagging her fingers.

Then she says, "I've missed you both. Now that you're both here, I'm going to roam all over this city by myself." Both the adult men beam at her with admiration.

From the pavement of the street, fifteen feet away, Hylas gives Zosimos a complicated look in which yearning, fear, and hurt are all stirred up and combined. "So, love," he says ruefully, "What does the name Zosimos mean, anyway?"

The harlequin returns the look with yearning and fear on his own face. "Likely to survive," he says.

"It means so much more than that, brother," David calls to him giddily. "It means likely to *thrive!*"

"I'm just not sure what we're doing together," Hylas says in anguish. "And I'm going to need to go back to my houseboat soon. I need some time alone."

"We are getting to know each other," Zosimos says gravely, putting his arms around the other man's back as they stand there, on that clean, bright street that used to house the prison. "And I want to see your houseboat, Hylas, so much! Spend as much time as you need, I'll come when you call me. Please do call me."

Hylas lets out a breath. "I'll keep you posted. Don't know how much time I'll need." But he tips himself back finally into the harlequin's arms.

The author and E, from some distance away, lie on a hammock, embracing.

Falhófnir eats the grass curiously, chewing some from one patch and then trying some from another, as though he were reading a book and comparing passages. Then he looks up, curiously, as though he'd suddenly gotten the news. He moves slowly up to Mala and brings his right flank to her, inviting her to run her hands through its plush black nap. After she explores his side with her fingers, she turns to the others.

"The divine mother is recuperating well. The hook popped

out of her just now, and she gave birth to a bouncing fresh new Donnaville. It's what we're living in right now."

Anna, unexpectedly, is crying. "I was afraid of what would happen to her." Then she stands next to David. "You really surprised me, old man, and I thought I would never have a good surprise again. I've missed you. I'd really like to bake and drink wine with you again."

David closes his eyes for a minute, feeling as emotional as a 50-year-old man who suddenly discovers he is pregnant. "I haven't baked anything all week. More important, I never had a friend like you. I want to cook you something, Anna, that tastes more delicious than anything you've ever eaten."

Then Kleine gets up from the grass, strides over to the harlequin, and softly ruffles his hair. "You and me, my friend, will always, every couple of days, have a standing date for lemon Diet Cokes, pizza, and popcorn. Sometimes my girlfriend, Anna, will come and comfort you, too, as much as you need."

THE END

ACKNOWLEDGMENTS

Many people helped me with this book. I am beyond grateful to my friends who read my drafts and gave me feedback: Ann Darby, Laura Kruus Reissman, Sean Monagle, Eileen Kelly, Shelley Marlow, and, always and everywhere, Karen Lippitt.

Two gay men were marvelous midwives to this book. I would like to thank the magical Michael Broder, publisher of Indolent Books, for his faith in me, and for always empowering writers. And I would like to thank David Groff for his splendidly helpful editorial suggestions, and for being such a decent human being he makes decency exciting.

Patrick Califia graciously gave me permission to use two lovely items from his short stories: "Your Father's Oldsmobile," used as a nickname for a character, from "It Takes a Good Boy (To Make a Good Daddy)" and a certain metaphor about regarding the sun as one's enemy, from "The Calyx of Isis."

Alexandra Devin provided much of the original inspiration for this book. I can't thank her enough.

Karen Lippitt has been granted the key to the city.

ABOUT THE AUTHOR

Donna Minkowitz is the author of the memoirs *Ferocious Romance*, winner of a Lambda Literary Award, and *Growing Up Golem*, a finalist for a Lambda Literary Award and for the Judy Grahn Award from the Publishing Triangle. A former columnist for the Village Voice, Minkowitz's writing has appeared in *The New York Times Book Review*, *The Nation*, *Salon*, and *Slate*. She is the recipient of a GLAAD Media Award, the Exceptional Merit Media Award, and the Award for Outstanding Journalism from NLGJA: The Association of LGBTQ+ Journalists, as well as an Art Omi residency.

ABOUT INDOLENT BOOKS

Founded in 2015 as a home for poets over 50 without a first book, Indolent Books today publishes innovative, provocative, and risky books by a diverse and inclusive range of writers across genres.